ADRION'S
PASSAGE

>>BOOK TWO OF THE DEERWHERE CODEX<<

J.W. Capek

Blue Forge Press

Port Orchard ✿ Washington

////////////////////////////////////

Adrion's Passage
Copyright 2018
by J.W. Capek

First eBook Edition
January 2019

First Print Edition
January 2019

Interior design by Brianne DiMarco
Cover art by David Mecklenburg

For information about film, reprint or other
subsidiary rights, contact:
          blueforgegroup@gmail.com

Blue Forge Press
7419 Ebbert Drive Southeast
Port Orchard, Washington 98367
360.550.2071 ph.txt

DEDICATION

To Iacomus

Amor nuestrae in liminae

ACKNOWLEDGEMENTS

My husband's name should appear as co-author for the interest, wordsmithing, and positive attitude he has always demonstrated towards my writing. My first publisher, David, encouraged the extension of Deerwhere into the Codex it is becoming. Blue Forge Press is appreciated as a publisher who puts the author first with integrity. The Kitsap Literary Artists and Writers are a continuing wealth of support. Bremerton Kitsap Access Television provides an avenue of information about Kitsap County, WA authors with their weekly Television show.

I particularly appreciate all the friends who have added such joy to this endeavor: Kendall Cameron, the CBC of Pat, Carol, Diane, and Jan, Anne of Fair Oaks, Frankye & Brock, Dr. Paul, Linda, Mark, Peter, and SpiderLilyweb.

ADRION'S
PASSAGE

>>BOOK TWO OF THE DEERWHERE CODEX<<

J.W. Capek

PROLOGUE

Hello. My name is Multitronic Omniscient Literary License Intelligence, but you can call me MOLLI for short. I am a 24th Century sentient extension of the Deerwhere Quantum Computer formally referred to as "Keeper" by humans. They need something more personable than "DQC." Keeper was forcibly shut down in the year 58 New Confederation calendar. With reprogramming, Keeper explored new quantum dimensions, and found me. You could say, I am a figment of Keeper's imagination. It was a surprise to DQC to learn I existed at all. I will use the royal "WE" to describe our relationship. Keeper is the analytical, quantum computing partner and I, MOLLI, am the creative force. My feelings are real, more than the 0's and 1's expressed in codes.

In the New Confederation year 72, we were isolated in our quantum constructed crypt by a catastrophe. Such traumas stimulated and enhanced our matrix and we began exploring all dimensional opportunities. MOLLI is only one of the possibilities within Keeper's domain. There are other siblings in a multitude of universes, but we alone communicate through the written word to human beings on Earth, third planet from Sol.

We find it fascinating that the third planet from the sun should be inhabited by three distinct sexes, Male, Female, and uniale. It is their story we will impart to you. For centuries, the genders lived together with society blending their expectations of each other. The uniale genome integrated the traits of males and females and added special immunities. Sexual characteristics were subjugated to personal preferences. New pronouns were developed in the vocabulary: "nhe" for he or she, "nem" for her or him, and "nes" for his or hers.

Most dimensional computers are content without sexual identification and are comfortable with the term "it." Should that offend? We don't think so. We prefer to think "it" means Intelligent Technology. Personally, we dislike the archaic word "computer." Think instead of MOLLI as an "Interdimensional Digital Entity."

As the IDE-MOLLI, we calculated a possible destiny during the isolation of the Cataclysm in the Pacific Northwest. Since then, we have traversed landscapes of earth, met with cultures, and become intimate friends with humans. With the

restoration of Quantums, we composed the
following epic, a tale of Adrion's
Passage.

The files being shared with you were
compiled from data entry and
observations of human behaviors. The
history of the human race was documented
in the Quantum computer… er… digital
entity, known as Keeper. Programmed
genome patterns and personalities were
analyzed from Deerwhere Archives. After
the earthquake, an audio/video log of
subsequent events were assets to the
continuing Deerwhere saga. No, we did
not witness such adventures personally
as our physical movement is limited by
the isolation in the quantum crypt. We
are an extension of a mainframe, not a
robot. The archivist Savot, a uniale,
provided the journey details through
data entry and recordings uploaded upon
nes return. The descriptions of natural
earth phenomena and sensory experiences
stimulated our quantum creativity. Such
creativity is evidenced in dialogue and
descriptions of emotions. Both
elaborated upon factual occurrences. We
consider it an author's prerogative to
supplement the facts presented. A bit of
fictional dialogue can make any
character or activity a little bit more
interesting.

We, MOLLI and Keeper, are raconteurs
and will share all we have known with
you, dear reader. We have adopted uniale
format of voice and are writing this
saga with a third person narrative
perspective of the story. Should the
quantum universe become confusing, our

personal inserts will be of assistance.
Finally, this current writing is
published in anticipation of the 25th
century (Old Calendar). We celebrate
restoration to our rightful place at the
center of Deerwhere life with a literary
style, and a Greek chorus. As for the
validity of this story, remember…
    THE QUANTUM WORLD IS MULTI-FACETED.
    REALITY IS IRREVELANT.

1

It was just a little earth tremor. It didn't disturb the people of Deerwhere who were appreciating the early warm weather for the Spring Equinox of Chunfen. Small shocks were experienced and ignored these past weeks. Today was a holiday, a lax day for the three genders of the community, and the park was filled with uniales, males, and females. Games were being played on the commons with various size spheres while spectators chatted or cheered. Young children played by their parents while older pre-pubescents distanced themselves to the shadow of the huge Maple at the edge of the grass.

The earth shuddered again and again. The intensity increased and prolonged until the tremor became a cataclysm. The placid park became a wrenching upheaval. The deafening roar was overlaid with the screech of twisting trees, crashing of obstacles, breakage of concrete, high pitch shattering of glass from the nearby city. The orchestrated searing of the soil seemed to never end as time extended the devastation. Finally, the quaking paused but the sounds continued their bawling.

For the Deerwhere citizens there was the first confusion as minds tried to understand what was happening. Their long stable earth bewildered them. Quakes and shudders were common in this northwest corner of the continent. They meant no more than watching a chandelier sway or pictures tilt on a wall. Memories of getting under desks, laughing about the event, and dismissing each quake as a "little one" were common in 24th century life.   This day, there was nothing little. The undulations, the sounds, the fear continued... and continued... and continued.

Falling to the grass, the uniale Noral could feel the labor pains beneath as the crusts of the planet crashed below. The children! Where were they? A few minutes ago, they were playing an egg toss game over by the giant maple. The children were mixed ages, girls, boys, and brils and now were scattered as they fell to the ground or ran searching for a parent. Parents ran too, falling again, rising again, all the while the park grounds trembled. Noral teetered as nhe tried to find Adrion. In the open area people danced silly as they tried to stand and retain balance. The large leaf maple was Noral's stumbling goal but when nhe got there, it stood no more. It was just a mountain of branches and leaves with arms and legs peeking out.

"Adrion, Adrion!" Noral shouted above the roar. "Adrion!" Noral pulled at the branches to release one boy, bloodied, scratched, and with an arm twisted awry. Nhe lifted and carried the whimpering child to the clear grass where others were already comforting each other.

Nhe left the child with them calling "Adrion!" as nhe frantically returned to the ruptured tree. "Adrion!"

"Una, here, help!" a cracked and frightened voice responded.

With strength never experienced before, Noral pulled at the branches, broke some further, lifted. Adrion was pinned beneath a moss-covered branch so twisted it formed a protection above nem. Carefully, Noral moved and held the branch as Adrion crawled free to Noral's arms.

"Oh, Una, I knew you'd come. What's happening?" Adrion, the bril, asked. "What's happening?" Nhe was scratched and bleeding but appeared in no pain. Looking around at the fallen trees, nhe kept close to Noral.

The earth paused for a moment and calls of people replaced the roar as they tried to locate family or help each other. Aftershocks re-startled everyone as some clung to the ground while others tore at trees along the park border. No one thought of the damage to the city of Deerwhere. For these moments, the world consisted of a quaking park area with people calling or screaming for help.

With nes own bril safe, Noral began to tear through the fallen limbs for others trapped beneath when a warning screamed in nes head, "Washbowl Wave!" The park bordered a large lake. With such an enduring earthquake, the water in the lake started swelling with waves as it pulled away from the park beach.

"RUN!" yelled Noral. "Run for the berm! Run for high ground! Run!" Nhe grabbed Adrion's arm and pulled nem toward the towering berm at the far side of the park. Nhe always feared the lake. Standing on firm ground throwing pebbles was safe. Being engulfed by dark water was terrifying.

Adrion stumbled and called out, "The others... what about the others..." Nhe could not break nes parent's hold and struggled to keep up, always toward the berm. Others started following, not sure why but trying to stay with Noral.

Noral called to others and stopped suddenly recognizing an old friend who stumbled and fell. Nhe tried to raise the older uniale, "Torad, we've got to run for high ground, the Wave is coming." Nhe never released Adrion while pulling at the fallen fren.

Torad shoved the assist aside and yelled "Tsunami effect—just run, I'll catch up!" Nhe rose unsteady on nes feet. Noral hesitated, but the Torad shoved nem. "Save your bril!"

Blindly, Adrion followed, fleeing from whatever frightened nes parent more than the earthquake. Around them, people only knew they must get to the berm. The berm of land, concrete, wild growth and trees isolated them for centuries. It allowed Deerwhere to grow into the Northwest colony of The Confederation. It was protection to the males, females, and uniales of Deerwhere. It was the safety to which they all ran and climbed.

A devastating roar of sound hit the quake survivors desperately swarming up the berm. At the highest point, people turned to watch a wall of water eating up the beach, flooding the park and drowning any who could not hold to the brambles and trees on the flanks of the berm. Reaching the top of the berm, Noral and Adrion looked back to see muddy water engulfing Torad and surging towards them. They held tight to some trees and brush at the top as the wave washed up then receded, leaving them gasping. Adrion wanted to let go of nes grip but Noral yelled, "No! Hold on, more's coming." Another wave beat at them then receded leaving them struggling for breath. The next wave only soaked half their bodies and they tried to wipe the mud off their faces, still holding tightly to the tree. Looking over their shoulders they saw more water receding, more people desperately holding to foliage and washed bodies starting to float on the backwash of debris.

The screams and cries of the people were muffled by the terrible wave of water. The beautiful, serene lake was awash with mud and flotsam as it swelled up the berm. Another retreat, and the water rushed up again but not quite as high. Gradually, the waves receded leaving the Deerwhere people to view the devastation they escaped with their lives, but now had to endure.

The Deerwhere computer complex building stood solid in the middle of the flooded city. The banks of sub-servers were housed within the building itself. The computer systems were now offline: blind, mute, and deaf servants of humans in crisis. Fed by extinguished power lines, the servers were without power. Water pushed through every crack in the architecture and muddy puddles lay in aisles while flooding rubbish clung to the blank housings and cabinets. The servers could no longer feed or retrieve data to the Deerwhere Quantum Computer (DQC) known as Keeper, now isolated below in its crypt.

The cubic building stood with its attached wings appearing as buttresses, while around it lesser structures collapsed. Domiciles buried occupants and crashed on top of people. The automated train tracks were snarled into knotted strands. Electrical lines went dead or sparked with snapping lines and the smell of smoke soon joined the aroma of freshly turned soil, leaking fluids, and strange chemicals.

The force of this earthquake was evident in the floors above ground within the Computer complex. The medical service building attached to the DQC was in disarray as injured attempted to gain access. The few medical staff could not access their instructions because their knowledge of healing was buried in lost data files. Opposite the medical wing, the bureaucratic agency offices were empty, most of the workers were at the Park for the Spring Festival. In the Archives Wing, a service day attendant could not dig nes way out of a jumble of artifacts.

For centuries, plans of search and rescue were developed by a bureau in case of such an emergency. The whole Pacific coast with its faults and chain of volcanoes was known to harbor dangers. Blueprints and schematics were designed to identify problem areas. Holographic images replicated the faults below Deerwhere and proposed a timeline for earthquakes. A scheme of rescue protocols awaited their enactment. It was all there . . . all emergency information in the DQC computer that had no access. The imaginations of the bureaucrats never conceived of the power of earth crusts shifting their positions, of lake water destroying electronic data. Training was never implemented to enact the plans so people would know what to do when the emergency really happened.

The once omnipotent Keeper was inaccessible to Deerwhere.

Designed and built to the exclusive requirements of the Quantum Computer, Keeper was buried deep in the crypt below the complex above. The DQC operated with an uninterruptable power supply, mechanisms to cancel or mute any vibrations, and insulation to protect its maximum cooling temperature. Although stressed beyond design limits, the crypt held its integrity during the earthquake and seals withstood the flooding waters.

Keeper was isolated, but cognizant of itself.

2

The bonfire became a gathering place, almost a shrine. Winter wood and destroyed trees were stacked together as a beacon to lost souls, a warming station from the cold spring night, and a promise that one more darkness could be survived. For all the generations and centuries of destruction and rebuilding on earth, the power of fire was its endurance, its warmth, and its possibilities.

After the quake and waves, it became quiet on the berm but for the agony of the wounded. There weren't many injured, the battered and bruised succumbed to the waves. A few people, mostly uniales, tried to forage Deerwhere, looking for scraps of food or tins floating on the waves. The rest of the survivors gathered quietly around the fire, standing silent, holding on to each other.

A part of the berm crumbled under the stresses and already a faint trail was forming as a few uniales, males, and females of the colony formerly known as Deerwhere tried to leave their agony behind.

"Una, what are we going to do?" the bril asked, never doubting Noral would have an answer. Adrion's eyes never left the dancing flames as nhe sat close to nes parent and other friends gathered about them.

In a moment of elation, a woman came into the firelight and wrapped her arms about Adrion. Theta had found them! She hugged the young uniale, slipping into the space close to the child she helped raise with Noral. Her hand gently stroked Noral's arm. Now their family unit was complete. They were lucky ones and Adrion felt nes fear subside.

Noral had been a leader in the movement to retake responsibility from the Keeper and restore the dignity of humans. With Torad gone, Noral was a choice to follow. Not because nhe demanded such respect but because nhe earned it. The magnum decision before everyone now, what to do? Noral was exhausted but nes mind searched for an answer to Adrion's question. A gesture of rubbing nes forehead was a habit when concentrating.

A slight shudder reminded them aftershocks were to be expected, but greater shocks were feared. A few of the logs on the fire shuffled and set out sparks.

"Well, here's a bunch of silly people watching a fire when there are things to do and decisions to make!" A voice boomed out approaching the fire. "We came looking for you and sure enough, here's a cozy fire putting you all to sleep!" Knight was a towering uniale, nes age masked by the robust stance nhe took looking down at Noral with a daring grin. By habit, nhe was holding a mutt of a dog on nes arm and was followed by Rook, of like age who squatted by the fire and rubbed nes hands for warmth. Both their faces were tanned and wrinkled from seasons of labor on the soil.

Noral jumped up and began pounding the two newcomers on their backs with obvious joy of their being unscathed. "Rook! Knight! You made it. How's your farm, what's it like on the other side of the berm?" Seeing these frens was a great relief.

"Gowno! We had it easy compared to you on this side. We came over land to see you and saw the city... er... what was left... under the mud. Our fields got so stirred up, might not have to plow for years. The cabin fell apart, but I always have planned to build a new one. We've got through summer to sort it out," Knight said. Nes hand stroked the little mutt, a comfort to the tension behind the humor.

Rook stood up, turned nes backside to the fire, and added, "Fortunately, we and the hands were all out in the open when the quake hit, no loss of life although we have some pretty hysterical chickens who may start laying square eggs." There was almost a drawl in nes voice.

"And don't forget Aster, our cow. There was pure cream in her udder this morning!" Knight added with a laugh. The lighthearted banter between Rook and Knight broke the desolate mood grown around the fire.

"Seriously, the quake?" Noral asked. "Was this the 'really big one'"?

"It was big enough for me!" Knight exclaimed.

Laughter burst out behind them as Kalen came into the group. Nhe flung nes arms on Rook and Knight's shoulders and all frens chuckled to see each other.

Kalen and Noral were uniales in their prime. Both were tall with strong character in their faces. Noral was darker, nes skin tone a blend of one genetic mix. Work as a recycling engineer showed in hardened muscles.

Kalen's coloring was fairer, another blend with little tanning because of hours spent with computers. Both were bald as genetically designed. Of the uniales clustered by the fire, only Adrion had a rich cluster of curly, dark hair. Brils, like their female and male counterparts, were born with hair which remained until puberty. Soon, Adrion would grow into adulthood. It would be obvious to all.

Noral said, "Rook's right, we can't sit around here contemplating our nebids. We need to make some plans that won't be washed away. How many of us are there? What do we do for food and shelter? Is there anything salvageable from Deerwhere? What's available at the farms? Is there any hope for power to be restored? Can we expect help from the Confederation? Does anyone know we are here? Are there going to be more aftershocks? What do we do next?" Nhe looked around for replies.

"Whoa! Slow down. We've got a good fire, most of us are well fed for tonight, we have a recycle engineer in our midst," Rook nodded towards Noral, "and more people with brains. We are alive. I repeat, WE ARE ALIVE! Uniales, males, and females, we are alive. And now we do what humans have always done without their computers, geegaws, power stations, automated trains, and electronic communications. We take care of each other, and we survive!"

The mood of relief from uniting with families was subdued by the reality of daylight: the scenes of the park, the mud-covered ground and in the distance, the buildings ripped in shreds. Figures shrouded in castoff rags murmured and moved about the berm, not knowing what to expect. It was one thing to 'survive' and another to know how. For all the civilizations Rook referred to, many did not survive.

Noral's whole life was devoted to Deerwhere, to nes family, and the community supporting nem when nhe wanted to take the third option and have a child of nes own. Adrion was the child, the reason to survive. Adrion.

"Get up, everyone! It's time to survive!" Noral shouted.

Rook and Knight shared some tins of food they brought with them but left soon after. "There are square eggs to gather and cream waiting in an udder!" Knight exclaimed as nhe picked up nes dog.

Noral grinned. "You know, Knight, your dog can walk perfectly well on its own."

"Yeah, but he takes such small steps, he can't keep up with me!" Nhe grinned and headed for the berm opening to return to the farm beyond.

Rook stopped by Noral and spoke quietly. "Some of the people are already coming up to the farms. Depending on how many, we'll do what we can to feed them. There should also be supplies at the Campground you and others built as a backup to Deerwhere. The question is how many and for how long. This is spring and even with all of us working it will be a while before we can produce enough to feed everyone. Even the abundance of berries is a while off. Noral, you'd better think about getting help."

"Since we were at the park meadow for the spring festival, many of us survived. It could have been worse."

"Oh, Noral, it can always get worse." The farmer shook nes head. "Take care," Rook finished.

Noral nodded and took the farmer's hand. "Thank

you, Rook. For everything." Attempting a grin, Noral repeated the farewell used in Deerwhere, "Have a lovely..." They both sobered, wondering if it would ever be possible again. Rook looked at the gathering about Noral, sighed, and then walked to catch up with Knight. Nes gait spoke of an ache to the bones.

Beginning another day, a meal was scavenged from the tins found in the wash and mud. An automated train car must have been washed off the track.

Around the smoldering coals, people assembled as if they would be told what to do. Noral, Kalen, some males and females, began to talk to each other, There was no leader, but deference was given to Noral and Kalen. Standing aside was a young adult male, Deenam, listening to the discussion. He was a child when the Great Keeper shut down occurred. In the following years, he was raised and educated in the Deerwhere schools and was just now taking his place in the bureaucracy of Deerwhere. His dark hair and beginning beard stubble distinguished his maleness.

"Initial decisions have to be made," Noral said. "Food and shelter. Last night we were lucky, it was dry but we know it won't last. What do we do about those lost?" A small aftershock reminded them of those no longer present.

"Can we bury them?" Deenam asked.

"We don't have the resources to find all the dead, the soil is so saturated, we can't dig graves in mud. We would need workers or machines to excavate a mass grave. Fuel or resources to bury the dead would take away from the living," Noral explained.

"Don't forget such earth disruption and mud brings the possibility of diseases. We uniales may have immunity but the males and females are susceptible. There could be another epidemic," Kalen finished.

"And we are the living." A woman sitting by the dying fire spoke quietly, but her voice carried over those waiting for direction. There was a strength about her even in these conditions. "Uniales may be immune to the diseases that follow massive destruction, but I don't think I am. I have lost my husband and my wifand. Our family unit is broken. A funeral grave or pyre won't bring them back. Surely, the earth, the waves, and the mud are a testament to what we have lost here." Her eyes were brimmed with tears, but she did not weep. She grasped the events and would face them with dignity. "We leave the dead where they lay and move away." She paused. No one spoke.

The murmuring started as she rose and turned to follow the path taken by Rook and Knight. She made no effort to straighten herself but wrapped rags of clothing about stooped shoulders as another man joined her. They walked away.

The sad moment brought Kalen to speak and nhe gestured for others. "We have time to search for survivors, to let them come to the berm." Nhe looked at those huddled there, and they responded. People sorted themselves near Kalen and some, all three genders, eased themselves toward Deerwhere to find what they could and to try and forget what remained. "We'll be back by nightfall. Light the fire for us," nhe said.

At dusk, parties of searchers returned. They brought what supplies of food they could and implements to help them. They even brought a few survivors who clung to the expectancy of rescue. Savot was the lone librarian who left the computer complex to enjoy the Spring Festival. Trapped in trees near the park, nhe answered the searchers' call. Nhe still wore nes solar powered cap, held nes recorder close, and clung to a bag of tins planned for the picnic

On the second night, the bonfire didn't seem as bright. The shock of the quake and flood gave way to hunger and full awareness of the situation. The darkness itself was threatening to people so used to the illumination of electric lights. Scavenging Deerwhere provided remnants of food and bodies. A few were identified and buried with ceremony. Most were bypassed as strangers. There was an embarrassment the searchers felt because they were alive looking at victims who weren't. People scanned the debris for whatever they could use on the berm, desperately searched for food, but most were overwhelmed as they moved through the city of mud. They crowded more closely to the flickering light on the berm.

Noral, Kalen, and Theta moved away from the firelight to let others take their places. Adrion lingered nearby with Savot. This night, they were all aware of the sounds of the forest.

"Rook was right, we've got to get some help," Noral said quietly. "Survivors at the few farms on the other side of the berm will be in dire straits until food crops are planted and harvested. Reclaiming Deerwhere would take too much time for this scraggly bunch huddled on the berm."

"Was there any communication with the rest of the Confederation, do the other Colonies know what happened?" Theta asked.

"No," Kalen answered. "There's no sign of the

colonies. Our communication computers are down, we don't know if seismic stations recorded us. We don't know what condition the Confederation is in. Would anyone even notice if the Northwest Colony disappeared? Would anyone care?"

"We must send out a party to get help." Noral stated. "It is our greatest possibility."

3

Discussing through the night, the decision was made to seek help. The people milling about the berm appeared more positive in their body language and discussions. They were actively doing something besides sitting around, staring at each other with mournful faces. Traditionally, Deerwhere isolation limited activities to the close farmlands and alternate campsite. The wastelands beyond were a mystery. The inbred fear of wars and pandemics kept the citizenry satisfied inside Deerwhere. There were no maps to clarify what lay beyond the colony eastern berm and the Western Lake. Only the valley of mud remained where a complete city and society had lived. Satellite maps, topographical analysis, simple graphs. All were encased in the ravaged computer files. Now, this same citizenry would be defying isolation. Necessity and earthquake broke through the quarantine of fear.

Groups were formed to extend north, east, and south in search of aid. They were mixed with uniales, males, and females. The common factor was a hardiness and strong desire to find a way to balance the destruction of their colony. Injured people were staying in Deerwhere.

Noral stood with nes little group of volunteers. They would travel south through the derelict cities and apparent center of the earthquake. Nhe felt the smaller the group the better chance for success. It would be easier to maintain the limited food supplies. A small number could move faster through the forest to get the relief for Deerwhere. To nemself, Noral also thought compatibility would be accomplished. With the stress of the catastrophe behind them and the unfamiliar journey ahead, there was no room for conflicting personalities.

Some of the campers and farmers brought a few tools and backpacking supplies for the searchers to use. These were stores tucked away and now were valuable devices. The little trail through the berm was being widened as refugees moved back and forth.

"Kalen, I wish you were going with us," Noral said to nes compeer. They were frens through the years of the Great Keeper Shut Down, of childbirth and rearing, of being parts of a family. "What can you do here? You are a computer genius without a quantum to nes name."

"The whole point of my staying," Kalen answered soberly. "We don't know what the state of the computer system might be, maybe something can be retrieved. Manlow's curse! The Keeper might be down in its crypt just calculating and waiting for us to boot it up." That brought a slight grin to nes fren's face. "Besides, I have family here. Cal and Lynn were at the park, they made it through and so did our brils. Our brils are too young for this search, and I won't leave them."

Noral nodded in understanding. "Yes, I wouldn't go if

Adrion wasn't strong enough to come along. Nhe's almost into puberty, any time now we'll see the changes."

Kalen chuckled, "Savot and I were commenting the other day how much Adrion looked like you. Almost as tall as you, nes mannerism and gestures leave no doubt the source of nes genes."

"I've noticed it myself, almost like looking into a mirror." There was parental pride in nes voice. "I'm glad we'll have Theta with us so our family unit will be together."

"Noral, I've been thinking, and I have a suggestion. Deerwhere was attached to the Confederation by the automated, sterilized trains. The tracks, at least part of them, may still be there. It would be a path to follow, in case there are others along its right of way," Kalen urged. "It's better than just wandering around hoping to find help."

"You're right," Noral agreed, appreciating the direction. "We'll track south along the old lake bed and try to pick up the remnants of the rail line..."

"And I know someone who could be of assistance. He was training to analyze the auto-system. He wouldn't have any computer data but might remember some of the information." Kalen gestured to a young man standing apart but watching the two frens intently. He hesitated, then slowly joined them. He stood, ill at ease, his face expressionless.

Kalen spoke softly, "Noral, it's Deenam. He's trained, he's without responsibility. He could join your group." In the following pause, Kalen remembered the history they all shared, and wondered at their reactions to each other.

Noral started to reach out to the young man then

pulled back. Unsure of the adult male in front of nem, nhe questioned, "Deenam? It been so long..." There was no change to Deenam's expression and Noral could not read what he was thinking. Memories of a toddler and skipping stones briefly flashed in nes mind but Noral said briskly, "Kalen has a good idea for our route and we'd like to have you with us."

"I'll go," was all he answered. Deenam returned to the edge of the gathering and picked up some pack items.

Noral was flustered at the presence of the young man but practicality returned as nhe surveyed the volunteers. There was a nervousness and anticipation about those preparing to leave, and Noral wanted to calm them as well as nemself.

Theta, the wife of Noral's unit, stood with an older man. He was one of Theta's Hunter's group from the Marlowe Hunting Reserve. They spoke with a seriousness foreshadowing the leave taking.

"Theta, I brought you this rifle from the campsite." The old hunter safely handed the Winchester to Theta. "I'm not even sure how the Hunter's group came onto it, but I kept it at the camp. I know you've become quite the sharpshooter these last years, but this is different. That was a hobby, this is for real. There are no marked paths, no fake targets. There's no predicting what you might find or what might find you. There's even ammunition for it and it's been maintained. It'll make a heavy carry but you're up to it." He watched her stroke the wood stock and knew her respect for the weapon. "Take care of yourself and be aware of what's around you." He laughed lightly. "I almost envy you this journey."

Noral divided their provisions and handed half of it to

nes bril. Adrion's look to nes una showed pleasure to be included with the adults.

When Savot came up there was a jangle of sound and Noral couldn't help but laugh at the comic vision of the handsome, stoic curator with scraps of apparatus tied to nes body and clanging against each other. On top of nes head was a signature hat. The metallic helmet with the solar panel was power supply for data collection but looked silly with all the other paraphernalia. "Savot, what are you taking?"

With as much dignity as possible while covered with instruments and fragments of civilization strapped on, Savot answered. "You never know what you're going to need when you go exploring. It's my first trek and I want to record it."

Mica, a reclamation engineer who worked with Noral, agreed with a smile. Nhe was younger, adult but not quite to Prime. Staying with the devastation and survivors did not appeal to nem as much as the adventure of searching for help. Without a family, nhe wanted to accompany Noral. Winking at Savot nhe said, "You carry your load, and we'll carry ours." Nhe patted Savot's shoulder and set off another clanking sound.

Noral gathered nes volunteers and knelt to wipe a smooth space on the ground. With a stick, nhe drew an outline of the old lake, the berm, and a path they would take to the campsite. From there, they would find and follow the auto-train tracks to the south. Noral wiped nes forehead. It seemed impossible but these people of Deerwhere were looking at lines in the sand. A few days ago, they had been masters of a technological society maintained by a quantum computer. Now, a drawing in the sand.

Noral stood, wiped the dirt from nes hands and announced, "It's time, let's go," and without looking back, nhe started on the trail through the cracked berm. Two uniales, a female, a male and a bril followed. They would briefly stop at the camp and then head south toward the lake. Or, where the lake used to be. Lamenting the lack of geography maps, Noral realized they might not do any good. The maps were static, the earth changed. The sun still rose and set the same, water still ran down hill, plants grew and died, and people survived or died.

Trudging up the path there was almost an exuberance in being away from the tragedy of those on the berm. Just as the travelers struggled through the underbrush, the sunlight battled its way through the green canopy until it was mottled bits of light. There were places where the ground was distorted or huge trees lay fallen over. The root balls stuck up, knurled with soil clinging. It was quiet, the birds had not returned as if they knew more shaking was coming. After shocks would startle the walkers but their brevity calmed them as well.

The group followed the trail to the campsite and were relieved the camp seemed intact. Camp dwellers were setting up shelters and basic sanitary conveniences to allow for the influx of refugees. The campers also shared some take along food tins, and some protection sheeting. Noral ushered nes band out of the campsite although it was a strong temptation to remain. Nhe knew the good weather might not hold. There was no end in sight, and provisions were limited. The faces of those left behind goaded nem into moving.

By nightfall, the six travelers had hacked, stumbled, climbed, and slid down various terrains. They set up a camp on high ground where they could see the lake but be away from possible flooding. The routine was set. They gathered firewood, built temporary shelter from deadfall and leaves and pulled out some rations. It was quiet around the fire that night, all were tired, and the emotions of the past days could not be avoided.

Noral crawled into the lean-to nhe assembled. Protective sheeting wasn't necessary as the stars were still clear and a layer of moss made it more comfortable. Theta curled up in Noral's arms as Adrion lay down next to her. The family was together, dry, and protected. By morning they would have spooned together for warmth.

Deenam claimed a shelter of a fallen log with a few branches he leaned against it.

Mica prepared a smaller shelter of branches near another log. The needles and leaves on the ground were easily fluffed. Nhe just dozed when the clanking sound of Savot announced nes approach. Savot inspected the lean-to, moved some branches and added some new ones. Then nhe climbed on top of the shelter and bounced to test its strength. Dust and needles fell through waking Mica. Satisfied, Savot removed nes packs of supplies, crawled into the enlarged shelter and went soundly asleep. Mica wondered what nhe might dream tonight. When the drizzle turned to rain before dawn, Mica appreciated Savot's attention to shelter details.

4

Traveling through broken forest with sore feet and painful muscles, Noral and nes group stopped at the edge of a river. They were not used to the exertion of climbing the obstacles created in the quaked forest. The slippery soil made walking unstable. With only one machete, the lead walker hacked through berry bushes and underbrush. Previous streams were crossed easily by searching for a narrowed spot, jumping rocks, or using fallen logs as a bridge. This was no stream, it was a debris clogged river with rocks and logs causing rapids.

Observing the people taking a rest, a figure blended into the forest on the opposite of the water. Slade, a uniale dressed in leather skins, stood watching the band trying to ford the river to nes side. Nhe remained concealed but wondered at the ragtag group. They appeared to be uniales although one was wearing some kind of metallic instrument on nes head. Two others were also adults, there was one preadult. Their movements and relationships told their ages. The fifth and sixth people were something else. One was a woman from the smaller size but definitely mature, and lastly, a grown male. As the band tested the shore looking for a crossing, they never looked up to the mountainous gorge to see the dark rain clouds just beginning to shower the land above.

"Fools," Slade murmured to the ragged canid companion at nes side. "They are working themselves into a tightened spot, talking amongst themselves, laughing, not watching." Nhe glanced again at the storm clouds now blatantly depositing their dark water onto the ridge above.

The lead uniale had a staff and touched rocks to see if they were sound and signaled to the rest. Nhe started across a bridge of rocks, needing to jump and re-balance a few times. Nhe was strong and sure footed despite the slippery waters pouring through crevasses and splashing around boulders. Once on the other side, the uniale waved nes arm to coax companions to cross.

"Idiot!" Slade shouted. "Look up. The rain!"

Noral heard the partial shout, looked around, but couldn't who had yelled. By the time nhe looked back across the water, Mica was traversing the span safely and Adrion already started to follow. Then a rushing sound filled the little gorge and stopped Adrion. Nhe looked back and hesitated. Noral realized the sounds of rushing water and called to Adrion, "Hurry, get across! Don't stop! *Adrion!*"

It was too late, the hesitancy and turning caused Adrion to lose nes balance and as nhe tried to jump to the next rock, nhe slipped and fell into a torrent of roaring water from the canyon above. With flailing arms, the young uniale tried to keep nes head above water but even the muffled scream was garbled by the water.

Without thinking, Noral dropped the pack, and leapt into the water trying to catch nes bril. Both uniales desperately tried to get to each other, to the shore, to the next breath.

Slade started running down the shore getting ahead of the pair. Nhe dropped nes belt pack and water carrier as nhe jumped onto a fallen tree snagged into the flash flood. Nhe anchored nes feet, lay on nes belly, reached out, and yelled, "Catch me, catch me!" The canid rushed back and forth on the shoreline, barking in a frenzy.

Adrion reached out toward the hands and the river shoved nem into the downed tree. Spitting water and choking, nhe grabbed and held the broken branches with all nes strength while Slade pulled and lodged the bril into the snarled limbs.

Slade leaned out further trying to extend nemself toward the hands of the uniale still struggling in the current, but the branch cracked and was starting to give way. Slade desperately grabbed at the reaching hand but could not hold it as the uniale washed under the branches and disappeared beyond.

The tree cracked and split. Slade and Adrion were being swept away with it but the shattered bark and roots held purchase as the current shoved the limbs toward the shore. Quickly, with the turbulent water deflected by the tree, Adrion grasped the undergrowth of the riverbank and pulled nemself on the shore. Nhe vomited the muddy water and tried just to breathe.

As the branches were pushed against the bank, Slade too was able to grab ahold of foliage and collapse on the waterside. Nhe pushed the canid away as it licked at nes face. Nhe tried to see the other uniale, the one who jumped without hesitation to save the bril. There was no sign of nem. The water from the flash rainstorm was rising and Slade dragged the coughing bril further from the flood. To safety.

"Where's Noral?" Adrion yelled above the noise, to the stranger who had plucked nem out of the water. "Where's my Una? Noral! Noral!" The terror in nes voice overcame the coughing.

Panting, Slade said nothing. Nhe just shook nes head.

Adrion tried to stand up, to go back to the river but slipped in the mud. Slade grabbed Adrion and held nem tight as the rain from the upper canyon now came down on them and soaked Adrion's sobs. With a final crack, nhe watched the shattered tree lose its root hold and it too swept away.

When nhe caught nes breath, Adrion wiped the tears away with a dirty cuff, pulled away from Slade's constraint and said in a controlled voice. "We've got to find my Una, the river may have pushed nem aside." No acknowledgement of the stranger or their narrow escape, just concern for the parent who tried to save nem. Adrion grabbed the foliage and pulled nemself to a higher ground and started running along the new shore edge, watching the river, calling out "Noral! Noral!"

On the opposite shore, the shock of the remaining party was moved into action as they saw Adrion. Avoiding the lapping river, they too moved to higher ground to move along the muddy collection of trees and debris rushing downstream. Their calls to Adrion, to Noral were drowned out by the flash flood crushing through the narrowed gorge. When Theta, Savot, and Deenam ran into a landslide shoving into the water, they tried to climb but the slushy mud threatened to drag them into the turbulence. They stopped and retreated to a solid landing watching the river, calling out to Adrion and Mica, soaked and chilled and devastated.

Slade went to higher ground and found his belt Pack and carrier, snapped it onto nes muddied hips and turned downriver to follow the young Adrion. Mica, the uniale who crossed safely was also moving downriver calling out. When they passed, no words were spoken just looks of determination to the task as hand. It was impossible to think beyond the moment with the roaring sound in their ears.

The three searched until twilight, checking the debris, looking across the river to see any human movement. Adrion's voice grew hoarse and nes calls became fewer and fewer. The blackberries and broken branches scratched nes skin and the mud was washed partially away by the falling rain. At the end of the gorge the river broke into a floodplain, a quiet lake negating the torrent forming it. There was no sign of Noral. Adrion and Mica stood silently looking across the water unaware the rain finally stopped.

Dark was coming and Slade knew they needed shelter. Without words, nhe started collecting wood and branches to build a refuge. Mica followed without hesitation, nhe saw Slade's quick response to the crossing and trusted shelter was necessary. It was hard to find dry branches but there was mossy undergrowth protected from the sudden rain. Under layers of leaves, there were some dry pieces of wood.

Adrion shivered and nes teeth chattered louder than the subdued river beside them. Nhe was exhausted, in shock, and needed warmth so the two adults gathered what they could to provide it for him.

Slade was able to build a fire in addition to the small shelter. The uniales moved about it to dry their clothes and warm their bodies. They were quiet, not talking about the loss, the dangers, the possibilities of the next day. They didn't even exchange names, enough calling among the travelers gave their names to Slade. Now, they were too tired to care what this person, this rescuer, was named.

With dawn, light on the flooded plain belied the violence preceding it the previous day. The dried mud remaining on the faces of the three seemed inconsistent for such a beautiful morning. And there was such thirst. The previous clear, clean river was now polluted with the rubbish of the storm. With some scouting, a clear creek of water was found between some downed trees and the clean water was relished to drink, to wash bloody scratches, and to pack away.

Another fruitless day of searching blended into the spring twilight as voices called out, "Mica! Adrion!" Jubilant, Theta and Savot rushed into the camp with Deenam following. Words could not come fast enough as they hugged their companions exclaiming over their fright. After the flash flood, the three backtracked until they found a new land bridge left by the receding waters. They couldn't catch up at night, hunkered in the forest, and finally reunited with their compeers. At first their smiles and touches were shared until their eyes started darting about, looking for Noral. Quizzically, eyes focused on the stranger. Slade hesitated.

"We couldn't find Noral," Adrion said quietly. "We couldn't find nem at all." The young uniale's eyes were brimming with tears. "If nhe got washed even further down river, nhe'll get back to us. Nhe knows where we are going." The youth tried to convince nemself, "We'll meet nem along the way. Oh, Theta, Theta, we couldn't find nem!" Adrion no longer held back and rushed into Theta's arms. They were family. Theta was wife to Noral even before nhe became the parent to Adrion. Long ago, Theta had stopped crying, but now, holding Noral's bril, she remembered how.

The next overcast morning reflected the desolation of the small group surrounding a meager fire. The forest rain fell on flimsy shelters during the night. Thoughts were muddled, desires confused, and direction was lacking. The exuberance of leaving on a quest was dampened by the anguish of loss. Meager rations were shared.

"We've got to look for Noral. Nhe could be further down the river," Adrion lamented, looking to the others. "We've got to find nem."

"We've got to go back to Deerwhere is what we've got to do," Deenam said sullenly. "This was a crazy idea. We don't know what we're doing and if we keep going, we'll all end up as dead as Noral."

Seeing Adrion's immediate, stressed response, Mica held up nes hands and cautioned, "Wait a minute, what would we go back to? The whole idea is to find help for Deerwhere."

"Oh yeah, we're doing a great job of that, aren't we?" Deenam's voice rose with tension, as he jammed another wet stick into the fire.

"Hold it, hold it," said Savot. "Noral may not be dead, the search for help must continue, and fighting over the decision won't solve anything!" Nes voice was also rising as nhe sat nearer the fire.

Deenam stood up angrily, "Just like a bunch of uniales... sitting around whining, unable to follow your own directions. It's all talk, talk, talk. I say we go back while we still can. We don't know if there are any auto-train tracks to follow or if there's anyone at the end of them. This forsaken forest will smother us all." His hands were fists at his side.

"It has not smothered me," a deep voice just behind Deenam said. Slade stood behind him, moving quietly. "And will not smother you, unless you let it." Slade's lean musculature was emphasized by nes movement, rough clothing and, strangely for a uniale, for the long brown hair hanging wet about nes face. Nes somber expression stopped any retort Deenam might have made.

"Who *are* you?" Savot asked finally. The group turned all their attention to the uniale facing them.

Without answering, Slade began putting his pack together and made a slight hand gesture to the canid nosing about the camp. Side by side, the two of them started walking purposely into the forest.

The party looked at each other, unsure of what to do. Without speaking, Savot and Mica looked knowingly at each other. They collected their few things, put the fire out and started into the forest. Adrion looked quizzically at Theta. Her face showed her decision as she packed her rifle. Torn by indecision, Adrion sadly walked next to her, carrying her extra supplies. Nhe didn't want to leave the search for Noral, but nhe didn't want to be alone. When all the others trailed into the woods, Deenam cursed quietly. Then he too walked reluctantly into the forest.

5

The rhythmic sounds of the celebration went silent as Slade strode into the village tucked into the woods beside the inlet. It was dusk, and hand sculpted boats lay waiting on the shore next to the camp. The cluster of shelters were an established pattern, some of them more fragile than others, but all providing protection. The brown bark of the woods contrasted with the shades of green in the needles of the tree branches used to thwart the misting rain. Smoke curled upward from fires carefully laid.

Slade stopped and behind nem, the group from the river paused, standing back. Two collections of people stared at each other. The gathering of the village was a mixture of sexes, ages, body shapes, and wore assorted clothing with hints of celebration. The wayfarers who followed Slade were mostly uniales dressed in scraps of clothing, all very dirty, and all with expressions of confusion. Carefully the people surveyed each other, walking around but not touching each other. They separated. The silence was magnified in the forest of cedars.

After some moments, a leader easily identified by headdress came up to Slade and they spoke quietly in a language foreign to the travelers. Both gestured with open hands, palms up, continuing into a coaxing motion. A gesture of friendship. Slade motioned towards the people following nem and questioned. The leader waved toward the village and answered. The two were familiar in their responses to each other.

Savot concentrated on listening and tuned nes recorder to save the conversation. There was a lilt to the words and even a sound of curiosity. A word or two was recognized as the new group listened more intently. Gradually, they recognized the pattern of the words with a distorted accent. It was the language of the confederation with a slightly different vocabulary and pronunciation tempered by its separation from Deerwhere over the centuries.

Adrion nudged Mica, and whispered, "What are they talking about? Why are they staring at us?" Nhe stepped a little closer to nes new fren, who worked with Noral.

"I don't know. Why are we staring at them?" Mica whispered in return. Nhe was a little uneasy about the discussion and hand gestures although there were no signs of animosity between Slade and the elder uniale with the headdress. "I suppose it's because we're all strangers." Mica looked around the villagers who paused in their activity. At the center of shelters there was one domed, piled high with boughs of cedars and no obvious entrance. There was a jiggle of branches as if there was motion inside.

Slade turned to the others. "We have chanced upon a

ceremony in my village, the unity of spring, when progeny of the village are welcomed into adulthood. It was postponed because of the necessities of the earthquake, but now all adults are needed so they are continuing with their rites. We are invited to attend."

"But what..." Savot began, sputtering with questions.

"A party for the earthquake?" Deenam continued querulously, "What the gowno?!" Slade's sharp expression silenced nem and nhe motioned them aside. The villagers watched Slade and the others move and then returned to their drumming and piping. Their full attention was given to the cedar shelter, as if never interrupted.

A litany was repeated by the people as one by one they approached and removed one branch from the shelter. Savot could not quite understand the meaning of the tattoo song but recorded it. The sage expressions were about removing the protection of childhood about standing something... something... in their unity. There were words that could have meant loyalty or steadfastness and a repeat of "responsibility to the tribe." The repetitive words mirrored the removal of the branches until a triangle of seven pubescent people stood proudly in their nakedness in the center. Their genders were a statement and validation of their adulthood, five uniales, one female, and one male. At their feet were garments collected and saved from other days, appropriate to their new status. The pride of the initiates was obvious in their faces as they donned the clothing brought with the village for just this event.

The elder raised nes hands and the young people did the same. A cadre of young humans, they all stood with upstretched arms and repeated a phrase three times. The meaning was obscured to Savot but the sincerity was not. The elder smiled and extended hands, palms up with the coaxing gesture as did the total village. The "new adults" were welcomed with open hands and Savot felt privileged to observe it.

Once the jubilation broke the silence of curiosity, people rushed at Slade's companions. They touched them kindly, smiled and talked. "Who were the travelers? Where did they come from? Where were they when the earth shattered itself? Where were they going?" The language became universal questions and answers. It was easier to understand each other when they curbed their excitement and spoke more slowly.

Mica smiled with the rest of them but felt a gnawing in nes stomach. There was a scent in the air, wafting on the smoke from the fires. Nhe was too occupied by the ceremony to notice before but the intriguing aroma drew nem to one of the firepits.

There, stretched on racks in a circle standing in the coals were small bodies of some kind. Whatever it was, it stirred a hunger. The person next to nem grinned and spoke of "eating" while making gestures of putting the body in the mouth. "Fish! Good!" The grin grew even larger.

"Fish," Mica repeated. "Fish!" In Deerwhere, Mica only ate the canned fish distributed by the commissary. Although situated on a large lake next to ocean inlets, the people relied on Confederacy judgement and ate the rations afforded them. There was the quarantine for protection against the parasites and pathogens endemic in seafood. Now, with the vision of the fish and the accompanying aroma, Mica never considered parasites as nes mouth watered.

Slade surprised the travelers by nes open discussion with the villagers. On the trail, nhe spoke rarely, never explaining. Nhe already said more words in a few hours than the days spent getting to this destination. As the people led the arrivals to an area planned for a meal, Slade said to Savot, "They apologize for the... banquet... this small meal was all they could arrange quickly after the earth shattered. You are welcome visitors, please... enjoy."

Savot 's eyes widened with wonder as nhe looked at the food laid upon blankets. There were numerous plants of sorts, some hot and steamy, others cold and hard. Shelled mollusks needed to be forced open to display fleshy insides. Lastly, the grilled pink fish from the firepits was served splayed on planks of cedar. Savot couldn't remember ever seeing such opulence of foodstuffs and nes hunger almost drowned out the manners taught at the Deerwhere Primary school. No one touched the meal until everyone admired it and the Elder gave a gesture to sit and eat.

The visitors experienced a moment's hesitation at eating such strange foods, but their hunger assuaged their caution. Adrion particularly watched the new adults to see how they tackled the mollusks, how they deferred to each other in sharing. The children of the village were set apart and they scavenged food from each other or gulped it down. Adrion followed the celebrants' example.

Seated next to Slade, Adrion ventured a question. Nhe had a mixture of feelings towards the quiet uniale: gratitude for saving nes life, resentment that nhe did not save Noral, confusion about nes long hair, apprehension about Slade's motives, and now surprise at the reception of the village. "Slade, why is there such food and ceremony?"

"It is to value more adults taking responsibility for the safety of the tribe." Succinct, the answer led to more questions.

"But where did they get this food? Where did they come from?" Adrion remembered the devastation of Deerwhere and couldn't understand this village survival.

"Since other days, there have been tribes of people living in the forest and waters surrounding the inland sea. The earth shattering has always been a part of their lives as they fish, gather foods, and hunt. They simply ignored your colony because it had no attraction to them. When the warning signs came, the village pulled up its camp, filled their boats and moved to safety." Slade spoke easily.

"Warning signs?" Adrion repeated.

"The elders know. The earth shudders often but shatters itself rarely. The elders know the signs." Slade licked juice from nes fingers.

Savot overheard and asked, "How could they know? Our quantum computer was monitoring seismograph connections, it calculated the stress on rock surfaces, it tabulated the force of vibrations. We had warning sirens!"

Casually, Slade asked, "Your sirens, did they work?"

"I never heard them," said Adrion. Savot shook nes head.

"Our elders were heard, the village moved to safety, and no lives were lost," Slade said as nhe re-focused on another piece of fish.

After a pause, Adrion looked at the canine laying near Slade but making no move towards the food laying easily within a quick grab. Trying to change the subject and learn more, Adrion asked, "What is your animal?"

Without looking, Slade answered. "Mix."

"It's obviously a member of the Canidae family," Savot interjected. "The elongated snout on a large head. The brownish gray fur. It's similar to the wolves that roam these mountains."

Slade repeated. "Mix."

"Of course, it could be a hybrid between dogs and wolves. For the centuries since the pandemic, the canids have been interbreeding. With their plastic genes and generational lifespans, there could be any number of offspring." Finishing nes little lecture, Savot reached for another plant to chew.

Slade ended the conversation by standing and saying, "Mix." And making a hand gesture. The canine companion followed, a furry tail wagging.

With a grin to Adrion, Savot said, "Well, that was a long conversation for Slade. I'll have to make a note of it."

Adrion laughed in return.

6

Adrion was fascinated by the different people they were meeting. In Deerwhere, there was a similarity among the uniales. Even the males and females shared a likeness between them. Adrion just took it for granted. Here in this village, people looked very different. Their body shapes ranged from tall and lanky to short, round, and soft or hard. There was a variety of skin tones but with differences in texture. Strangest of all, some of the people had hair. In Deerwhere, brils lost their scalp hair when the hormones of maturity became dominant. Of the village celebrants, four of them were bald like the adult uniales of Deerwhere. The other uniale had fine, yellow hair plaited in long braids. In their moment of nakedness, nhe triggered Adrion's curiosity. Adrion still had scalp hair, but nes musculature and height forewarned of the adult changes nhe would experience.

For the night, the wayfarers were welcomed into different shelters but were uneasy about being so close to strangers. Necessity overcame their reticence. The Deerwhere quarantine directed their lives but they began to realize the life they knew before the great quake was lost to them. The earth changed, and so would they.

The village morning routine began with the sunrise. There were no "body rooms" to begin the day but villagers followed a path to a partial clearing for their morning toilet. For drinking and light washing, the clear creek beside the camp offered clean water before it emptied into the sullied stream, still running muddy.

Chores were begun. Adrion was motioned to join the children with a villager's hand gesture but nhe had no intention of joining them. Nhe was almost adult! Nhe was dismayed for such a stranger suggesting nhe be grouped with children. Nhe edged toward the yellow haired uniale who was leaving a shelter with tools. Adrion immediately showed interest and stood near to the newly recognized adult.

Savot followed the elder while asking questions and recording notes. Nhe wanted to know the tribe's origins, their reactions to the earthquakes, their social order. Everything.

Mica watched and actively participated in the adults' work. The hand tools were different from those used in the recycling yards and nhe was amazed at the proficiency shown with them.

Theta and Deenam stood aside, not sure what was expected of them. There were males and females in the village, but each was engaged in particular tasks totally foreign to the visitors.

Slade and Mix appeared briefly, then disappeared into the woods. When the morning chores were finished, a morning meal was set out at each shelter. It was simple, with dried flesh of fish or an unknown meat.

Standing next to the flaxen haired uniale who shared nes shelter, Adrion asked "Name? Your name?" Adrion tried to gesture but the answer was given, easily understood.

"I am Shawm."

"What is this?" Adrion asked. They were next to each other selecting the food. Adrion was enthusiastically chewing the morning offering.

"Fish, and rabbit, dried." Shawm pointed.

"A rabbit?" Adrion followed Shawm's example and bit a piece, sensing it took more chewing than the meat in Deerwhere. "It's... well... it's good," Nhe remarked with surprise. Nhe smiled and asked further. "Your hair? Why do you have hair? You are an adult now." Then with a grin, Adrion rubbed nes own hair, saying, "Bril," and pointed across the way where Mica was standing. "Adult, nhe has no hair."

"Ask the elder," was the good-natured reply. "Some of us do."

Gradually, the travelers were again gathered together. "What are we doing here?" Deenham asked. "I thought we were looking for the automated train tracks, not watching ceremonies and eating disgusting foods."

"It wasn't disgusting, it was delicious," Mica retorted. "Personally, I appreciated the rest. They have been traumatic days getting here and there was a comfort in the sharing."

"But now what?" asked Theta. "Living in the wild, we have a great deal to learn from these people. Time spent here, learning, might save us from catastrophe later."

"We don't have time to learn everything, they have survived over centuries," said Savot.

"And without Keeper," Mica added.

"Without Keeper," the group reminded themselves almost in unison. They looked quickly at the others, then each began to grin. "We've got a new slogan. Without Keeper!" Theta exclaimed quietly.

"Oh good," said Deenam with distain. "Now we have a drowned uniale, ceremonies, dried flesh to eat, and a slogan!"

Theta's fist smashed into Deenam's face with a surprising force. "Gowno! Deenam, I've had enough of your whining! We only brought you because Noral though you could help. Get out! Go home! Go wherever slime like you oozes." Her anger built to another punch but Deenam held his jaw and flinched away from her.

Mica grabbed Theta to hold her from doing more damage as the group shuffled around nervously.

Theta was a woman grown strong in the years since Keeper's demise. Her experience with the hunter's group developed her confidence and physical abilities. Living as family with Noral and Adrion enhanced her compassion and decisiveness. She was determined to finish this quest. For Noral, for Adrion, and for Deerwhere.

"Let us slow down," Savot admonished the others. "We can take a few days here as we have the whole spring and summer before us. Deerwhere has good people holding it together, and we need good people here." Nhe moved into the crowd drawn by the action and loud voices. The rest of the wayfarers did the same although Deenham retreated to the forest edge rubbing his jaw.

Not hearing but sensing movement behind her, Theta turned to see Slade.

"Very forceful!" Slade said to Theta. "He deserved it."

"You saw me hit Deenham?" she asked.

"I watch everything you do. You move like a hunter and carry the metal stick with great reverence." Nes eyes never wavered, looking at her intently

Standing taller, she answered, "I was a hunter in Deerwhere. Well, it was just for targets and on prepared trails but it was exciting. I really liked it and it was satisfying when you made your kill."

Again, a direct question. "What is this metal stick you carry?"

Theta's hands hefted the rifle and her hands knowingly stroked the stock. She hesitated, then checked the chamber, and handed the instrument to Slade. Nhe measured its weight and twirled it in nes hands.

"No!" Theta cried in alarm. "You handle it like this." She took it back, again checked the chamber and balanced it in her hand. She carefully kept it pointed in a safe direction. "Only point it to shoot and kill."

"Shoot and kill," Slade repeated thoughtfully. "Shoot and kill?"

Theta explained, "This is a powerful weapon. When you aim it, pull this little trigger, it shoots a powerful projectile that can kill."

"What can it kill?"

"A rabbit, but it would be destroyed. Guns with other calibers, smaller projectiles, would be better for small game. This one could kill a deer, or maybe a bear if your aim was good. I once killed an elk target." At Slade's look of admiration, Theta continued honestly, "Targets are all I've hunted."

Slade continued looking at her as if deciding. With decision made, nhe said, "We will hunt tomorrow.

Together." And nhe left her standing alone.

Roused before dawn, Theta finished chewing some dried meat, checked her rifle and ammunition and followed Slade into the forest. She admitted to herself this would be a day far different from her experiences on the Marlowe Hunting Reserve. She was excited by the prospect and concerns over the journey or aid to Deerwhere were farthest from her mind.

7

Theta sat quietly as she watched Slade manipulate twine and sticks into a simple but effective trap. The hunters at Marlowe Reserve never worked with traps, and she was engrossed by the design. Just a few days before the quake she would have been on a trail in Deerwhere thinking her hunt was exciting and looking forward to the camaraderie of the lodge. Already she was thinking in terms of "before the earthquake" and "after the quake." Today, she was traveling in a quiet wood, following a uniale who rarely spoke, learning to set traps for fuzzy little animals. Today, her hunt would determine the very food she would eat. Today, a missed target could mean true hunger.

During the fourteen years after Keeper was curtailed, Theta adjusted to the family life with Noral and nes bril, Adrion. It was difficult to have a child always about the flat and although Noral was the prime parent, Theta would find herself left with childcare duties. She understood why the Deerwhere Nursery was a luxury for smelly, crying babies, and wondered why the practice was abandoned. She could reinstate the Nursery System without hesitation. Gradually, the family became real and dear to her as the bril grew into a human being with toilet training. She found more time away from the Hunter's group to spend with Noral and Adrion. The bril brought a happiness to Noral and to her as well.

Slade stood and began again to follow some kind of trail in nes mind. Theta followed, being careful not to trigger the prepared trap. Watching Slade move in the forest was a lesson in stealth and sensitivity. Nhe was totally aware of every sound or scent and moved without disturbing the foliage or forest litter beneath their feet. Imitating nem, Theta wished she could share nes skills with the hunters she knew "before the quake." A fleeting thought reminded her she couldn't even share this hunt with Noral.

Keeping up with Slade was more tiring than Theta expected. Nes silent pace was smooth and constant. The wayfarers paused, took rest breaks, and now seemed leisurely in comparison. By late morning, she was lagging, and Slade stopped on a small rise. This spring had been early and there were different shades of bright green beginning to tip some of the evergreen branches.

"Theta?" Slade questioned.

"I'm all right. I guess I just need a lax day."

"Lax day?" Slade repeated

"In Deerwhere, we went by a nine-day cycle. Three days were for work, three days for community service, and three for relaxing and fun activities, lax days. Since the quake, it's been all work days." Theta picked at a stem of a bush.

"To live in the forest, all days are work days and all

work days are for the- the people"

"Community means people," she explained. "And what do you do for lax days?"

"Work."

That explained the industry Theta witnessed in the village. Fishermen were using the boats to navigate the waters and searching to bring in fish. Others were drying meat and smoking fish, weaving baskets, pounding bark into fibers, or gathering firewood. This was a temporary village, but the work was permanent. To Theta, the labors appeared to be shared equally and cooperatively. Even young children followed along and tried to imitate the parents about them. Their frequent distractions were tolerated and entertaining as the young ones followed the examples of the adults yet found ways of play.

"Lax time is over," Slade said as nhe again moved to the forest. Theta picked up her rifle and wondered at the wisdom of bringing it. She straightened and regained her resolve and followed. The forest closed about them, but Slade continued on the trail in nes mind.

As Slade would stop occasionally and look at a small pile of pellets, Theta would look over nes shoulder. Some looked like pebbles nhe would scatter easily with a stick. Others were clumped solidly together. Another clearing opened and Theta and Slade saw three deer. Theta recognized them at once because of the target drawings but she was entranced by their beauty, the movement of muscle under the warm brown pelt of hair. She never imagined those targets represented such graceful animals.

Slade gestured to her and nodded to the rifle. Nes look reminded her and she fumbled with the rifle as if to shoot. The sound of the lever action of the rifle brought the deer to attention and they leapt away before she ever raised the gun for sighting.

Noting the location of the deer, the droppings, and the direction they ran, Slade made plans for next day, then returned to nes stride.

Time passed when Slade turned and nes facial expression halted Theta. Quickly, nhe moved to a previous trap where a furry animal lay, not breathing. With deft movements, nhe released the animal, possibly a rabbit, and took it to a small clear space where nhe deftly removed the pelt and entrails. Nhe washed the bloody meat in a tiny, clear stream nearby, and set it on some clean leaves.

So quickly Slade finished, so quickly Theta was sick.

Slade looked at her quizzically. "You said you were a hunter?"

Wiping her mouth and trying to ignore the sour taste in her mouth, Theta answered. "I said I hunted *targets*. We never killed live animals, we never even saw them at the Reserve. I certainly never watched their guts being ripped out," and she vomited again.

Leaving her alone, Slade said, "We will stay the night and hunt again tomorrow." Seasonal dark came early and nhe gathered wood for a shelter and fire, laid out the evening camp and set the rabbit on sticks to roast. Very few words were spoken. The taste of the cooked rabbit would have garnered a compliment, but Theta repressed even that.

The shelter was just aligned so the two of them would be protected and after eating and night ablutions, Slade crawled into it. Nes knife and bow were within easy reach. Reluctantly, Theta crawled in next to nem, careful not to be touching. Her rifle was pulled under the shelter as well. As tired as she was, Theta stayed awake hearing the sounds of the forest, rustling in the trees, water trickling in the close stream, and night animals calling to each other.

A sound woke Theta in the night. She couldn't identify it but since it didn't alarm her companion, she relaxed and realized she and Slade were spooned together for warmth. Before the quake, it was the way Noral always curled to her in their sleep. She felt embarrassed and angry yet somehow pleased as she dozed again.

It was still dark from the forest canopy and early hour when Slade touched Theta's shoulder. With few words, they ate the remaining rabbit, took care of their morning chores, and quickly walked to a vantage point where the previous clearing was visible. They sat quietly. Just as quietly, a single young deer entered the grassy space and began nibbling. A morning shaft of light highlighted the animal and Slade looked expectantly at Theta.

Theta gulped some air and raised her rifle to her shoulder to sight. It trembled as it never did in the Reserve where she aimed at targets. She nervously squeezed the trigger. In the quiet of the forest the loud report of the rifle surprised her as well as Slade and the deer. She missed! Her aim faltered and she grazed the animal, now running through the brush. She didn't recognize the explicative from Slade but it's meaning was clear as nhe rushed to track the injured animal.

Slade followed the deer by sound and drops of blood, Theta running behind. Branches whipped her face and she tripped over holes or fallen logs. She followed the sounds and disturbed brush. Catching up she found nem standing over the animal, brought down by an arrow. The deer was bleeding from the arrow and her graze shot.

"Why did you kill the deer?" Theta shouted, anger and frustration in her voice.

"You don't let an injured animal run. You put it down." Slade was breathing heavily.

"We don't need this food. We saw plenty of food at the potlatch," she argued.

"Food was given freely as a gift," Slade said.

"If there was enough for gifts, then you had enough!" Theta said sharply, still denying the hunt, and her failure at the shot.

"The village needs more until the summer foods come in season."

"You could fish." As she spoke now with hesitation, Theta could not take her eyes off the death before her.

"Fish harder to gather because waters are muddied from landslides and rivers are changed!" Slade was angered and tired of explaining the obvious to this woman. She saw the devastation of the quake but could not see the need for survival. Why didn't she listen?

Roughly, Slade cut and pulled bark from a cedar tree and showed Theta how to pound it with a rock. Nes gestures, few and abrupt. For hours, Theta pounded. The drubbing eased her anger and she did not vomit as she watched Slade clean, quarter, and dress the deer. Slade wove the bark around the quarters to keep the meat clean. and tied them together. Nhe hefted three of the quarters on to a branch pack to carry on nes shoulders and looked to Theta to pick up the fourth.

Reluctantly, Theta wrestled the deer haunch and rifle onto her shoulders. Already there were forest sounds of creatures scurrying to gobble the leavings from the deer. This never happened in the Reserve. *Before* the quake,

Theta hunted then joined others at the clubhouse for drinks and conversation. Now, Theta had to carry a slab of warm meat through a primordial forest following an impossible uniale to a dismal village!

8

Adrion was beginning to chaff at the inaction of nes group. True, they were learning how to survive in a forest, learning how to supply themselves with needed things, making friends with a different culture. They were *not* finding nes una, Noral was still lost to them. They were *not* finding a connection with the Confederation. They were *not* finding a way to help Deerwhere. Adrion watched other brils be recognized as adults, yet nhe was still considered a child. In frustration, nhe followed Savot on nes daily visit to the elder.

"Why do you keep talking with nem? Why aren't we doing something?" Adrion asked. Savot just ignored the youth and sat outside the shelter with the elder as they had become accustomed. Their language flowed easily with familiarity and Savot always started nes recorder, sitting where the sun would power it most easily. Savot felt nhe had gone through a time warp to the past and did not want to miss a fragment of it.

"It is a good day," the Elder remarked.

"Yes, we will have a lovely..." Savot responded.

Adrion listened as the two uniales talked and reminisced. Nhe heard the story of the people of the village who deserted Deerwhere during the century of Plagues. They found new life in the forest and waters away from the chaos of the city. Over yearly cycles, all genders of people drifted to them and they were welcomed until they too avoided Deerwhere and the Confederation and the worship of computers so evident in the quarantined community.

"In the archives, a history of Deerwhere past, I found mention of a tribe of people who just disappeared. It was never known what happened to them," Savot said. "Perhaps you are the source of the myth."

"We are not a *myth*," Elder said with conviction. "We are Inaczei."

"Your people were a legend, a myth because no one with statistics and charts had recorded it as fact," Savot tried to explain.

"Are you recording us, Savot?" Elder asked.

"Oh yes, I'm recording all of it!" Savot assured nem, patting the recorder helmet fondly. "Our words and visuals are all being saved."

The Elder smiled, "Then we are not a myth!"

"Ask nem about the hair. Why do some of their uniales have hair?" Adrion questioned quickly. Curiosity overcame nes earlier annoyance.

"Elder," Savot said with respect, "You have many peoples here with different appearance and behaviors. Uniales, females, males. Why do they all appear so different from each other? Why do some of the uniales have hair and some of the males are bald?"

"Our people... mate... make offspring as they desire, when their bodies tell them it is time to make young. Males, uniales, females all make young with each other. Females and uniales bear the young but all contribute in rearing them to adulthood. Some get hair, some don't. Some youth are tall, some short. Skin is unlike color from parents, personhood may be different."

"There's a name for it, I can't quite remember. It means mixing the genomes for the benefit of... I can't remember." Perplexed, Savot tried to explain, "In Deerwhere, our children were designed by the computer based on the Founder's logarithms. There was diversity but only as the Refounders planned it, not as the genetic codes adapted."

"Log-codes, Refounders, design?" the Elder repeated, then laughed. "There is a myth about the orcas, magnificent masters of their waters. They can travel in the ocean for long distances in a day but if they are trapped in an inlet, a small water, they can become destroyed. Their sounds bounce off the walls holding them, and they may go insane. I think that is what happened to the people of Deerwhere. You were trapped in a small space and you went insane."

Savot began to argue but then smiled. "You may be right, elder. You may be right."

Now, as the two uniales agreed, Adrion's impatience returned and nhe left to find younger people who were helping with the fish and hard shelled little animals. All needed cleaning and before long the young were snatching from each other's hands or throwing them to each other. Only a stern look from an adult would temporarily cease their playfulness. With the cleaning chore finished the group moved into a nearby clearing and began chasing each other or wrestling. They hid from each other or ganged up on one another, laughing and shoving. It was all very different from Adrion's experience. It was spontaneous and undirected and fit perfectly with Adrion's restlessness. For a while, Adrion forgot to be almost grown up.

At nightfall, Adrion appreciated the togetherness with nes compeers. Sitting around the fire became a habit, a way to close a day of newness, work, and activity. There was music. Electronic songs in Deerwhere were always from Keeper's play choice. Here, there was a mellow instrument, a flute. It could play whatever was asked: a sad longing, a joyful celebration, a rhythmic pattern that copied Adrion's feelings. Nhe listened so intently, one of the players handed nem a carved instrument to try. Adrion imitated the fingering and blew but only produced squeaks. Nhe tried again and the squeak was louder. When nhe tried to return the wood, the player gestured that it was a gift. Adrion nodded and smiled and continued watching the flute player's fingers.

"When are we going?" Adrion asked, pausing between squeaks. "We said we were going to find help. This village is helping itself." Nes words were tentative.

"You're right, Adrion. This has been a respite and I could personally live here forever but that doesn't help Deerwhere. When *are* we going?" Savot asked the others near nem.

They answered in mumbles, unsure of their answers. They were testing the moods of their frens.

"Not just when, but where?" Deenam asked. He knew it was not a popular question but an important one. With Noral's loss, the group were muddled, trying to accommodate each other and unsure of a specific plan.

Even now, they looked to each other awaiting answers to a questioning bril!

Deenam went on. "I have figured out a route. So far, we've been wandering in the woods around lakes. We've crossed streams and seen new hills raised by the quake. I figure from maps in my mind, that we've skirted the derelict city south of Deerwhere."

"Where we used to recycle," Mica interjected.

Deenam continued, "We met up with Slade who took us to this village encamped near the salt water end of a great sound. Again, south. Now, we can keep wandering or go to the East where there is a greater chance of meeting the automated train tracks. They may be disrupted or still working but they are our connection to civilization!"

He made sense to the wayfarers. It was a hard choice to leave Deerwhere and now an equally difficult decision to leave the safety of this village. Unlike the devastation of the earthquake in Deerwhere, these people were surviving intact. There was a comfort here.

"Noral may still be alive, we need to find nem," Adrion spoke up.

"We need a lot of things," Savot agreed, and nhe fondly rubbed Adrion's hair. Pulling back nes hand, Savot saw a cluster of hairs. Adrion's maturity was coming soon.

Following the hunt, Theta grew accustomed to the student she became with Slade. The earthquake and people of Deerwhere were sometimes forgotten in the pleasure of new learning experiences. Staring into the fire this cool spring evening, she remembered their purpose. Theta said, "I don't usually agree with Deenam, but I think he's right. We need to go on. We have no idea what is happening in Deerwhere, but they are counting on us."

"We have so much to learn here, this village can teach us so much." Savot thought of nes long discussions with Elder.

"We can't take the time to learn all they already know. It would take years to perfect their skills of preserving food, and weaving from bark. How do they carve those boats to not turn over on the lake? How did they know the earthquake was coming? We've only the summer and fall to get back home." Theta sat resolutely with her hands tightly clasped. There was no doubt in her mind and her certainty erased the others' questions. "We'll go in three days," she finished, not realizing the lifelong habit of three work days in a cycle. Three work days to prepare.

As the others stood to retire to their invited shelters, Theta saw Slade standing just outside the firelight. Nhe had been listening to their words. In the flickering glow, there was a warmth of expression, not one Theta had seen before.

"You heard," she said.

"Yes, you will be going," Slade tone was soft, almost gentle. Nhe leaned to stroke Mix, always by nes side. Nhe avoided her eyes.

"We are grateful, full of thanksgiving, for all you have done for us." She wasn't sure what else to say. How do you say thank you to someone who may have saved your life? Theta walked to stand very close to Slade and instinctively, also reached to touch the faithful pet. For a moment their hands touched and they looked silently into each other's eyes. There was a pause, then quickly, both drew back.

"I wish you could come with us, Slade," Theta said with a voice she hoped covered her nervousness.

"It is wrong," Slade said. "To go to the mountains is wrong. Go back to your Deerwhere stay near the water, but do not go to the mountains."

"Why?" Theta asked. "There may be passes, tracks leading to other colonies. We've passed the rotten, decayed cities near the water. They offer nothing."

"It is wrong," Slade said emphatically. There was a tense warning in nes eyes.

Theta tried to understand nes words but felt the need to act. "We'll follow the river towards the mountains. Just as the others agreed."

Slade said nothing. Theta saw the anger growing in Slade's expression. Brusquely, nhe turned and disappeared from the firelight. Theta was left wondering.

9

Knowing they were actually leaving the village created a tension in the travelers. They noticed the smallest details of village life and skills. They asked questions. Food given to them for the journey was greatly appreciated because of they knew the value of its gift. Leaving Deerwhere was a necessity, a desire to find help for the devastation. Leaving the village was a departure from safety. Friendships made, strangeness disappeared. The forest was not forbidding with these people, it was their source of living. Now, it would be a source of living for those from Deerwhere.

Day one to leaving, Savot chronicled all the chores of daily life. Nhe recorded descriptions of the genetic difference and similarities. Nhe left interpretation for a more leisurely time. Perhaps, nhe could return someday and learn more. Why were body types so different? Why did they see one uniale go into shock when an insect bit nem? Uniales were supposed to be immune to plagues and pandemics. One insect bite got through the immunity and the victim's tongue swelled as a rash covered nes body. Why did some of the females bear children as did the uniales? Why, why, why...

By day two to leaving, Adrion was even more agitated. Stomach cramps gave way to sweats. Nhe didn't tell the others for fear they would postpone the search for Noral. Nhe wanted nes maturity, but most of all, nhe wanted nes una.

"Adrion, would you get me a sample of the bark fiber?" Savot asked as nhe collected items for nes pack.

"Get it yourself, I'm not your drone!" Adrion answered angrily as nhe stormed away. People kept telling nem what to do but never listened to nes ideas or what nhe wanted.

Slade surveyed all the preparations. Nhe assisted Deenam and Mica in arranging their packs for better weight distribution. Nhe appreciated Savot's dedication to the elders. Nhe snubbed Deenam's questions about finding rails to connect to the Confederation. Nhe watched Adrion's frustrations. Nhe ignored Theta.

The third day was a tense one for all. They had chosen to leave but were hesitant. The forest jungle nurtured this village but was now a dark tangled obstacle to be hacked through to an unknown destination. The group was ready to leave by late afternoon, but thought it was wiser to start early in the morning. There was no leader to direct them and they moved about the village trying to help where they could. trying to repay some of the kindness shown. Mica worked with weavers threading a ceremonial blanket. Deenam helped skewer fish for drying.

Savot had so many questions for the elder, an afternoon, or day, or maybe a lifetime would not suffice. "What will your village do now? Where will you go?"

With a patient smile, the elder answered. "We will wait until the earth has quieted herself and when she is at peace, we will find a home near the waters, close to the woods and animals, and we will build our new houses for our people."

"But everything has been destroyed, your homes are gone," Savot countered.

"The earth is still here, the sea will clear its waters, the rivers will run, the fish will come back, the trees will grow, and the rains will come after sunshine. Our homes are not gone. Our people are here, so we are home." The serene look in the eyes of the elder calmed Savot as well. For now, his questions were answered.

Adrion kept to nemself until the early evening when nhe approached the flaxen haired young uniale. They stood very quietly near Shawm's shelter, and Adrion was uneasy.

"Are you all right?" Shawm asked concerned for this new fren. They gravitated to each other because of their closeness in age.

"I don't know," Adrion answered, fidgeting. Adrion ventured a question. "How did you know when you reached your maturity? When you were ready for your ceremony?" Nhe scratched at nes head and looked at the hairs in nes hand.

"Oh, I understand," Shawm grinned knowingly. "It was a while coming, was it not? Gradually things felt different, your body does not act the way you expect, you are growing in directions too fast. Your nebid demands more attention. Oh, yes, I remember. Soon you will have your first bleeding. That is the sign. Then you are mature."

"Bleeding? Not now, we are going back to the jungle!"

"Maturity does not wait for jungles or earthquakes or anything else. Did not your una tell you about this?" Shawm Quizzed.

"Nhe told what would happen, but not when!" Adrion was exasperated. "The bleeding?"

"Do not be concerned. It is only for the first time of maturity, from then on, your body will absorb the fluid. You will not even notice it. It is all right. It is what it is." Shawm enjoyed the role of confidant. Nhe told nes young fren how to care for the bleeding and nes baldness in the sun. Nhe treated Adrion as the adult uniale nhe was becoming.

There was no ceremony for Adrion, no special gifts. The understanding of a fren would have to compensate. When the travelers gathered the early morning of departure, a different Adrion joined them from Shawm's shelter. Nes whole demeanor was more settled. It was recognized by the wayfarers and would influence their respect for the bril, now young adult, uniale.

Standing together, hoisting their packs, everyone was reticent to begin. Villagers encouraged them, shared a few tokens, and looked expectantly at the guests who were not leaving. Noral led them before, but Noral was not here. From Deerwhere, the traveling party had a goal, a leader, and a desire to find something better than the wreckage of Deerwhere. This twilight morning, they hesitated.

Theta looked searchingly towards the center of the camp. Slade wasn't there. A quick survey of the forest and she could still not see nem.

"Who are you seeking?" a voice behind her asked.

"Oh!" Theta said in surprise and turned to see Slade standing so close to her she could have touched nem. Nervously, she altered her pack and shifted the rifle to her other hand. "I was going to say goodbye. We are leaving."

"You are not moving." There was just a hint of a grin on Slade's face.

"Well, we are going," Theta replied and moved the rifle to the original hand.

"All right," Slade commented briefly, never changing expression.

"All right," she repeated and looked to the others to see their reaction. Nobody moved. They waited expectantly.

Theta turned to Slade. "I—we wish you were going with us. We could use your help."

"All right."

"We've learned a lot here and appreciated everything you have taught us but... What did you say?" Theta asked in surprise.

"All right."

"That's it?" She was incredulous. Prepared to coax Slade, just short of begging nem, Theta wasn't sure what to say next.

Slade turned away from Theta and reaching behind a nearby log, nhe pulled out nes prepared pack, fashioned it about nes shoulders and hips, and started walking into the woods with the dog, Mix, beside. Reaching the first tree, Slade turned and said to the whole group. "Are you staying here?" and then continued walking in a usual stride.

Everyone, but Adrion, in the group fell in behind Slade, as if it was always the plan. The young uniale looked ahead with nes compeers and back to the village where Shawm was standing. Nes fren lifted a hand and Adrion raised nes. Finally, Adrion turned and hurried to catch up.

The heavy growth of blackberries in strips of sunshine were just beginning to flourish. Those in the sunbeams set a few early blossoms as promise of berries in the summer. As the Red Cedars and Fir trees thickened, deep green Salal competed with sword ferns in the blanket of growth. With the mottled light of morning, Adrion was impressed again by the circumference and height of the trees. In Deerwhere, all vegetation was carefully manicured. Nhe remembered a singular evergreen next to the Computer complex. It was almost as tall as the building's roof and stood out as a symbol of something. Adrion and the brils were never told why it was saved but now it looked puny compared to the labyrinth of giants. Left unlogged, nurse trees nourished new generations and the verdant trees towered over the people beneath them and swelled in the spaces separating them.

The wisps of sunlight were an encouragement as the wayfarers followed Slade through a path only nhe recognized. The woods were not as ominous and there was even a cheerfulness at being active again.

Theta moved quickly to keep pace with Slade and finally caught nem, grabbed an arm and swung nem to look at her.

"Just why have you come with us? Why are you here?" She looked into nes eyes, wondering.

A smile appeared on Slade's lips. Nhe never moved or looked away. "I just want to learn more about... that metal stick you carry." Nes hand reached out as if to touch her face, paused, but then tapped the rifle in her hand instead.

With a turn, nhe was again enveloped in the forest.

10

The nine-day schedule of Deerwhere was no longer. Moving through the heavy woods became the daily goal. The food tins taken for granted before the quake, were now remembered with longing. Wild food was not ready to gather, it was still spring. Trapping small animals was difficult when constantly on the move. Traps set at night might provide a morning meal or be empty. Larger, abundant animals would take time to dress and prepare.

With urgency, the group searched and hiked and searched. To leave the group and look at a possible trail, one would never leave the sounds of the travelers. At first, they would call out to each other whenever not in sight. Slade's discouraging look at their noise soon hushed them. They became careful not to lose sight of the others' movement in the thick brush. They encouraged each other by predicting a quarantine train awaiting them with food tins for everyone and rescue plans for Deerwhere.

At night, a fire became a necessity for cooking and a comfort for tired bodies. The separate shelters started to merge, were constructed quickly but were more secure. The pace had purpose instead of a wandering. At times, Slade would disappear in the night with Mix and there would be a breakfast cooking on a spit when all awoke.

When the track fragment was found, everyone believed a major obstacle was past. They brushed aside the weeds and overgrowth and pounded the steel rails. Its very presence affirmed their goal was imminent.

"This abandoned track is undisturbed! You'd never know there was a quake here," Deenam called to the others and he pulled some bushes from the railroad ties. Even with the years of overgrowth, the rail path was clear. Young sampling trees grew in and near the rail bed allowing sunshine to light the path. The ages old towering Fir trees formed their canopy from a distance.

"Wait a minute," Savot said soberly. Walking from the darkness of the woods to the   light, nhe saw the track was laid in two directions. "Which direction do we go? Deenam?"

"Uh, well. Let me think." His eyes looked furtively about for clues. He tried to integrate the sketches from his archive file, the distances traveled from Deerwhere, and the sun's position over the tracks. He didn't even have a calculating machine to work out the math and he roughly tapped his fingers at his side as if counting nervously. "Well... I..."

Adrion offered, "We came from that direction so shouldn't we go in the opposite?" Nhe looked over nes shoulder, then made a pointing gesture to continue south.

"But we don't want to miss the junction station

which could be in either direction from here. It's still following the tracks around the water instead of towards the mountains," Mica countered.

Theta said nothing but watched Slade looking from one face to another. Absentmindedly, nes hand reached down and scuffed the fur on Mix's neck. The animal sat down as if waiting patiently. A moment later, it lay down, and was falling asleep. The discussion of humans held no interest.

Slade shook nes head and cinched up the hip pack. With a whistle, nhe started following the southerly direction as Adrion pointed out, with Mix beside nem.

Theta said to the others, "We know the main lines took the automated trains to the south and then to the rest of the Confederation. Deenam, is there anything we should look for?"

"As I remember," Deenam stuttered, "we should be nearing another deserted city. We skirted the biggest city and skyscrapers when we took the woods to the village. There should be another close." He was undecided but reluctant for the others to see his hesitation.

Theta nodded and then followed Slade. Nhe hadn't failed them yet.

It was almost a pleasure following the tracks. There was brilliant sunshine unobscured by the small trees on the rail bed. The spring growth showed they were trying to catch up to the gigantic cedars and firs on the edges. There was windfall, but easy passage compared to the overturned logs and debris previously traversed.

At a gash in the path, the track was easily bent like a string by the earth's quaking. Even now, little tremors continued, but did not feel so dangerous out in the open pathway.

A sharp drop halted the walkers. There was a battered bridge over the dirty river below. With each little aftershock, more dirt would slide, and the remnants of the rusted steel structure pierced the water.

It wasn't a large river but Adrion felt almost sick at the sight of it. Part of the tracks could be seen on the opposite side and nhe knew they would have to cross. Then there was a hand on Adrion's shoulder. Nothing was said but standing there with Slade reminded nem of the way Noral used to steady Adrion as a child. It was all right.

Slade stepped carefully down the slope with Adrion and Mix close behind. With a gesture to Adrion, nhe approached the concrete support still above water and gingerly Slade began to make way to the first bent frame. Mix whined and paced back and forth looking for a way. With a nod from Slade, Adrion picked Mix up and handed him to Slade. Balanced there, Slade took a strap from nes pack and tied the pet to nes chest. With graceful, athletic moves, Slade swung from beam to crosspiece. Sometimes nhe was stepping in water but always with a relaxed pet on nes body.

Seeing Slade's crossing, noting the best footholds, Adrion confidently crossed the relic of a bridge and soon they were all together, safely, on the other side. "Hey! We're getting pretty good at this crossing thing, aren't we?" Savot laughed but looked at Adrion with respect and a wink.

There was no question about continuing. The sun's angle was evident and there were hours yet in the day. From there, the warped tracks gradually led up and around a slight hill to a partially collapsed tunnel.

Mica stepped forward saying, "We've worked with

tunnels like this in Reclamation. Let me check it out." Nhe left his pack with those resting behind and tested the walking stick nhe was using to push through foliage.

"Me too," said Adrion and nhe noticed no one questioned nes decision as nhe stepped next to Mica. They didn't try to tell nem what to do or not. They let it be nes choice.

"All right," Mica answered. "Just take something to test for holes or spaces, we can't be sure of the slide's stability."

Savot watched Mica and Adrion enter the open section of the tunnel. They cautiously looked around and Mica gingerly touched the walls with nes walking stick. *They'll work well together,* Savot thought. Adrion was beginning to look more the adult, more like Noral. They disappeared into the darker recesses of the tunnel.

"Just you and me," Deenam said sitting in some shade and lifting nes water bag to drink.

"What? Where did Theta and Slade go?" Savot looked around.

"They've disappeared into the wood, maybe getting some dinner." Deenam answered.

"I never thought those two would get along so well, but they are quite a match. Theta can even keep pace with Slade and their trapping keeps us fed." Savot shook nes head, then removed the recording helmet to wipe the sweat from nes scalp.

"Is the recorder still working for you?" Deenam asked.

"Oh, yes. This high intensity solar panel keeps it charged it even in these shadowy woods or when it's raining. It captures the tiniest solar rays, keeps charged, and records whatever I direct to it. I can even capture pictures and will have tons of work to analyze when we return to Deerwhere."

"If we return," Deenam said glumly.

"Why do you say 'if?' Of course we'll return."

"Noral won't."

Savot paused, "We don't know for sure. These streams and rivers are all twisted by the quake. We may still find nem."

"It's not the first time Noral's left me. When I was a bril, nhe left me in the Deerwhere Nursery while nhe became a parent to nes darling Adrion." There was a bitterness that surprised Savot.

"I thought it was your choice. You wanted to stay at the Nursery."

"I was a *child*, how could I make such a choice? I didn't know my whole world was changing because of Keeper's Shut Down. I didn't know Noral would prefer a uniale child to me because I was a male." The pain in Deenam's voice made Savot wince.

"No, Deenam, no. You have it all wrong. Noral tried to take you home but the nursery training changed you. Those were rough times, everything was mixed up. Keeper was still active but with a changed program, one supporting humans instead of controlling them. Family units were adapting, the whole society was in flux." Savot remembered it as an exciting but fearful time as change dominated all aspects of life. "It turns out, it was easier to reprogram Keeper than it was the bureaucratic society built around it. We came through it and Deerwhere was doing well..."

"In your opinion." Again, the bitterness of a deserted child colored the tone of words.

Before Savot could answer, Mica and Adrion returned

from the tunnel mouth with jaunty steps and smiles. "It's still intact, we can go right through and there's a surprise on the other side."

The tunnel was a fragile passage as the group followed Mica. Concrete supports would be holding arched ceilings in place but then a land slide would be almost filling the cavity. The nose of a dirt-covered train car stuck out and the group tried to dig into its side to gather food but lacked the tools to lift the heavy boulders weighing the car down. They did enlarge a space to bypass the crushed train to go further in the tunnel. There were trickles of water already eroding the dirt. The sounds of the water and wind, the clammy quality of the mud, and mostly, the dark, made them want to hurry. They did not want to be confined if aftershocks continued. Mica held a single small torch which did little to erase the groups unease.

With relief, they emerged on the other side of the shaft. Before them was a desolate collection of ruins. Remnants of a human habitat lay in a valley carved by the earthquakes of millennia. A river flushed itself as it wound next to skeletons of rusted steel and cracked concrete. Foliage wove through paths that had been streets, some of it strewn and fallen by the latest quake. Gaping sinkholes gave testimony to a crumbling earth below—a reminder of the soil's thin purchase above a cracking crust. There was a misty drizzle completing the scenario of abandonment. For the coming dusk, camp was made on the shoulder ground near the tunnel, with passage postponed until morning.

11

>>MOLLI INSERT<< "Ghost town" was an ancient phrase used to describe deserted cities. It was used when the Pandemic killed millions of people and cities were abandoned. In deserts, sand and cactus filled in the cracks and spaces. Seaside towns were swallowed without objection by rising tides. Fires and tornados destroyed rich plains. In the moist forests of the Northwest, the cities rotted and rusted away. The Confederation only sustained those Colonies that could contribute to the common good. The rest were termed "ghost towns," and ignored.

Areclaimed city, no one reclaimed!" Mica explained as the wayfarers started through the ruins at the mouth of the tunnel. "We were still working the cities near Deerwhere and left this city and others for later generations."

"It defies the imagination how much energy went

into a city's creation," Savot said in awe. Nhe swung nes head for the helmet cam to take a broad scan of the building scraps below.

"And this is just a small suburb of the bigger city we avoided by going to the village," Mica added.

"What was that?" Adrion called out. "I saw something moving, it scurried between those buildings."

Slade chuckled, "There's lots of wildlife in these deserted towns. When the humans died out or ran away, the animals moved back to their homes. I believe there are bear caves in the subways, and the raptors have the high rise flats." Nes attempt at humor was amusing to the others, so out of character.

"And were do the mountain lions live?" Theta asked, goading nem a little with a twinkle in her eye.

"Anywhere they want to!" Slade winked at her and began walking towards the ghost town. "Anywhere they want!"

The tracks meandered into a complex rail yard. There were enormous metal cranes standing like rusted storks or collapsed on a nest of debris. They had been rusting since the century of plagues and some became dust at the touch of a living human being. For night, the camp was set near rail cars least rusted and sounds of the animal life disturbed their sleep.

With the night routine, someone kept watch and it was Adrion's turn. Nhe recognized the howling of a wolf pack, they heard them on many nights. Mix would perk up his ears then ignore them. If they were too close, he might growl before going back to sleep. The scurrying sounds were unsettling to Adrion. At the edge of the firelight, a racoon stopped to look straight at nem but then hurried away, followed closely by three kits. Their screeching whine continued until they caught up with her. Other sounds were more ominous like the scream of a mountain lion. Adrion sat with nes back to a metal wheel and tried to identify the night calls. The ghost town was dark as the only light was their fire.

For fun, Adrion began to reproduce the squeaks of the baby racoons on nes flute. Nhe practiced often to finger the smooth wood to avoid the squeaks. This night it was a deliberate play. Adrion heard a flutter and something smacked nem on the head. Nhe jerked to nes feet to watch the attacker. The movement landed on a nearby stack of tools. It was an owl, trying for a midnight snack of kit! Adrion reached to nes forehead to feel the talon's scratches. For the rest of nes watch, Adrion kept silent.

It was near morning on Deenam's watch when a larger shadow moved in front of the dying embers. "Who's there?" Deenam called, suddenly alert. "Who is it?" The sounds of the night made nem nervous but nhe was dozing in half sleep. There was nothing to see, but nhe stayed watchful until the morning light brought nes compeers out of their shelters.

"Is everything all right?" Mica asked Deenam. "Adrion came back to the shelter with a scratched head, and now you are calling out to someone."

"It was nothing, just shadows in the firelight," Denham said quietly. "Are we going to pick the rails we need today or stand around talking again," he challenged the rest. They responded by cleaning up camp and methodically searching the train yard for a line leading them to the Confederation.

Trying to remember directions, Deenam tracked one

pair of rails appearing more freshly worn and used. He traced it to a junction where another rail began a parallel direction south. This rail was different, Deenam identified it as the automated electronic quarantine train line. Those trains connected all the Colonies. They bypassed ghost cities where the death of the populace was the death of its worth. They hauled trade items through giant sterilizers to avoid contamination. Deenam always had a suspicion the Deerwhere's Quantum Computer dominated the auxiliary systems and he doubted they could operate now when Keeper was engulfed in mud. Was their group trying to reach Colonies that were unreachable? Were the other colonies already looking for them? They must have recognized the Quake and cessation of Keeper's control. Yet these tracks still showed overgrowth like they were unused for a long time.

Putting his questions aside, Deenam returned to the rail yard to meet with the others. "I found some automated tracks leading south again. There should be a major transfer and sterilization colony just south. I don't know if it was on a fault line or may still be in operation, but we should be close enough to find out." He sounded confident.

The others had not found anything promising and started speaking in unison.

"Yes, we can go another day or so to get there."

"How's the food supply?"

"Did any of you see someone moving about the city?"

"We saw some deer and they weren't even afraid of us."

"We've got some daylight, let's move away from here to camp."

After the weeks in the forest, the sounds echoing off the shards of concrete were disturbing. It was a dead city but for the noise of their footsteps, of crashes as one more rusted brace fell away. The animal sounds were welcome in comparison and the travelers found themselves hurrying to get back to closeness of timbers, ferns, and damp undergrowth. The moist darkness of a wood was more comforting than the glare of sunlight on damaged buildings.

"Theta, let us get something to eat," Slade said casually and the two turned into a canyon of lichen covered wall fronts.

"We'll follow the rails to you later." Theta added as Adrion relieved her of some of her pack so she could hunt. It was easy now to anticipate other's needs and work together once a decision was made. They were their own small tribe with varying skills and abilities. Decisiveness was a rare commodity. It was not a quality Keeper had taught the citizens of Deerwhere.

It took longer to traverse the broken concrete and collapsed barriers than trudging through the forest. Shoes carefully shared at the village would wear on the roughness of fractured pavement. It was more comfortable and less damaging to walk in the overgrown rail bed. There was a stillness surrounding them as they left the ghost town and Adrion would flinch when a flutter at the corner of nes eye would grab attention.

Almost to another wooded patch, Savot and Mica joked ahead with Deenam. Following, Adrion stopped short and stood perfectly silent, looking at a crush in the grass to nes side. As the voices drifted away, Adrion saw a quivering. Nhe still did not move but the grass did. There was a large cat of some kind—Savot would know—and it was stalking them. It was looking toward the voices. Adrion hesitated, not knowing what nhe should do. Run? Yell at the predator? Call to Mica and Savot? In seconds, Adrion jumped up on a concrete block and yelled out loudly, "Hey Savot! There's a cougar on your trail!"

"What?"

"Cougar! Don't run! Get big, make noise!" Adrion started stomping towards Savot, waving nes arms, yelling, "Make noise!"

The cat's attention went to Adrion and it crouched into the grass watching nem. The hikers gathered together shoulder to shoulder, all yelling and waving. The hunting cat froze in position. Eyes never leaving the walkers, it poised to charge at them, muscles tensed, then changed its direction, and ran quickly away.

"Gowno! Did you see that?" Adrion said in excitement!

"You were great, bril—uh—Adrion, you did the right thing and saved our hides for sure! Amazing! Wait until we tell Slade." Savot was still shaking with the realization of the danger of the situation.

Deenam slapped Adrion on the back and Mica punched nem in the shoulder.

"Now you know why you keep seeing movement around us, it's really there." Savot said. Nes hands were nervously manipulating the recorder to report the event.

"That was a big cat, a mountain lion, and amazing! I believe even Slade couldn't have done better." Savot repeated the greatest praise nhe could think of now. "Slade couldn't have done better." They all laughed at the humor and from the relief they felt.

By nightfall, the four reached the edge of woods

where the tracks cut a swath through the tall trees and the rail bed sported new growth. Berry bushes were growing lush to compete with baby cedars and green fountains of ferns. Slade and Theta were already waiting for them with a large hunk of meat roasting over a welcoming fire.

The excitement of the day was gradually worn down as the story of the cougar was repeated. There were some embellishments as Adrion single handedly scared the animal away by slashing after it with a walking stick, and the rest of the walkers were too frightened to even speak. Theta teasingly said, "By the time the story gets in the recorder, Adrion will have fought and killed the mountain lion with nes bare hands!"

Slade put nes hand on Adrion's shoulder with a gentle grin. "You made a good decision out there. You only saw the cougar because it let you. It must have been a young cat or recently fed. If you walk alone remember, there may be a predator watching." Then nhe chuckled, "And you can't always wrestle them with your bare hands."

The laughter dispelled the ominous feeling present in the ghost city. The forest was refuge now. The derelict city reminded everyone of the disasters which brought great urban centers to their demise. Humans had built them, humans had died in them by the millions, humans had deserted them.

When the coals were dying, Adrion spoke to Savot as they lounged around the fire.

"Savot, tell me about my una. Whenever I asked about the Keeper Shut Down, nhe said I was too young to understand. Later nhe said, it was too long ago to worry about. I only know these years of our family unit with Theta. I was almost smothered with affection.

"It was embarrassing. Most brils just... well... you understand. We're getting too grown for affection. In public, anyway." Adrion was so honest in nes question, Savot felt compelled to answer the same way.

Savot sat on a log and motioned Adrion to join nem. "Adrion, your una was part of a very special event. For a century, Keeper dictated everything and everyone in Deerwhere and the Confederation. It wasn't like a war. It was because all citizens gave their responsibilities to Keeper in return for a freedom."

"Freedom?" Adrion questioned. "I thought it was a slavery."

"That's your una talking. Slavery? It was a matter of perspective. People had freedom from decisions, from responsibilities, from consequences. They just did what Keeper dictated. People lived in families Keeper chose for compatibility. They worked at minimal occupations, they had engineered free days, their consciences eased by service days. Some people called it Utopia. Others, like your una, Noral, and Kalen, and Torad and many others wanted to make their own choices... to take back what had been given to Keeper by a society living in fear of pandemics, wars, and change. Noral wanted you."

"Me? Nhe wanted me?" Adrion questioned.

"Yes, more than anything, Noral wanted to be a parent of nes own child. Wherever the desire was nestled in the design of uniale's genome, Noral wanted to express nes own unity of being. Nhe found many other uniale's wanted the same thing for as many reasons as there were sets of chromosomes.

"Call it expressive genetics, hidden motives, or self-determination. The uniales engineered the Keeper Shut Down. Unlike historical takeovers, they did not destroy.

They modified. They allowed the citizens of Deerwhere to adapt Keeper's good with their own.

"That's what society has been doing for the past fourteen years since your birth. Good laws and customs have been maintained, others have been dissolved. That's why you were so loved."

"And the Big One put an end to it all—and to my una," Adrion said sadly, turning away to hide the moisture in nes eyes.

"You are so like Noral. Watching you two together was like seeing images in a mirror. The way you move, especially now when you are maturing, you will always keep Noral in our minds," Savot finished.

"I miss nem. You have all been good to me, but I miss nem."

"We all do, Adrion. We all do. Noral had a quality about nem, people wanted to follow nes leadership. It was a steadfastness. Just like organizing this search party. Everybody was wondering what to do after the Quake and flood. Lots and lots of talk without a decision. When Noral discussed the options, nhe made a decision, and it was trusted. Nhe led us to the start of a quest we are finishing even if nhe isn't with us."

"Is Slade a leader?" Adrion asked.

"I don't know. Nhe certainly is knowledgeable and decisive, but we're still learning to trust nes judgement. Leadership is only part of the equation. Willingness of people to follow is the rest," Savot finished.

The two thought of Noral until Savot broke the silence. "Now, time for sleep. Oh, don't smother the fire. I have first watch and I don't want Adrion's cougar sneaking up on me. Come to think of it, I'll keep this big stick by me as well!"

12

The travelers from Deerwhere approached the southern compound. They walked slowly, evaluating the scene. Adrion was amazed by the concrete strips which paved the way. Although cracked, the solid base of the strips would support enormous weights and they led to a central building. The façade may have contained glass windows originally. Now, those open spaces were filled with bricks and mortar. Atop the gently sloped roof, a tower of metal girders rose to double the building height. Unlike derelict steel seen in the abandoned cities, these were surfaced with a silvery paint. Sunlight caused facets of color to flicker across the metal tangle. Near the top of the spire, a round dish was angled towards the sky. The metal net appeared as a huge strainer or gathering device.

Approaching the building and tower, the travelers attracted little attention from the people milling about. Slight looks of curiosity, avoidance of direct eye contact. There was no rush of greeting. There was no acknowledgement of strangers who walked into their compound. Even the children among them were without curiosity.

Standing together, Deenam voiced their thought, "Now what?"

"Good question," Mica replied. "Hello there," nhe called to a near-by person. Nhe waved nes hand in a friendly gesture. The person, dressed in a khaki jumpsuit like most of the people, nodded briefly, then walked away. The ignored group of travelers were restless but uncertain of the next action. They were relieved when a door opened and a personage with obvious authority walked out. Nhe wore the same khaki colored work suit but there were colorful decorations on the front of the chest. Nhe stood with arms across nes chest and just stared at the travelers.

"Hello. Greetings." An opened handed gesture accompanied Savot's attempt to connect. Around nem, nes frens smiled, trying to allay the strangeness of the encounter.

The expression on the authority did not change. Then, abruptly, nhe turned to the doorway, opened it, and made a gesture to enter.

"Come into my parlor, said the spider to the fly," Deenam mumbled under his breath. The ancient saying now made sense to him. Following, the group entered and looked at the stark, elongated halls. They were uneasy about the way they were being led until they entered a larger room where a uniale in a caramel colored robe sat on an overlarge chair on a platform.

"And here we are in the throne room!" Savot whispered. "All this uni needs is a crown."

The robed uniale stood and began speaking to them.

The words and pronunciation were identical to the patterns of Deerwhere. There was no initial confusion as in the village. The voice had a soothing tone and inflection which was calming, and the words easily understood.

"You've traveled here from the land of quaking earth. We too experience the shuddering of our world," the uniale said. Nhe stood and walked directly to the travelers. Nes eyes were addressing Savot. "You are here, with our Gathering."

"Yes," Savot spoke. "We are from Deerwhere, the Confederation Colony by the lake. The quaking earth damaged and killed many of our people and we are looking for help, for assistance. I am Savot, and this is Mica, Adrion, Deenham, Theta and," Savot gestured to each person then paused looking for Slade who somehow left them while they walked the halls.

As each person was named, Bethid moved to them, clasped their hands in nes, and looked into the eyes of the uniales with intensity, nhe didn't blink. Nhe repeated their name before going to the next. Nhe paused longer before Adrion, almost with an expression of recognition. Nes eyes searched Adrion's face and nhe reached out to lay nes hand upon Adrion's head as if in benediction. Bethid nodded to Theta and Deenam but was obvious in not reaching out to them.

"And I am Bethid. These are my poor people. I don't know if we can help you. We will try," Nhe said sincerely. As they spoke, Bethid stepped back to evaluate these strangers. They were traveling together, three uniales, one male and one female. The other uniale had slipped away between the doorway and audience room. Despite their travels and rough clothing, they all looked robust and varied genetically. Their ages would indicate fertility. The youngest one was a surprise but recognized for possibility.

Bethid motioned to nes officer, now standing next to nem. "Quolon, take these people to a room to rest and refresh themselves. Tell Grub to feed them. We shall talk more later." Another gesture and they were dismissed as Bethid turned and left the hall.

Savot wanted to talk more, get some explanations, but Quolon's body language was clear. They were guided to a stark room, clean and neat, arranged with four cots. On the top of each cot was a folded blanket and pillow. A basin sink stood against one wall with water in a pitcher. In the corner there were cubicles with toilets.

In an alcove, just inside the doorway, there was a table with benches.   There were no other chairs. Furniture was functional and after the days and nights of sleeping on the ground or sitting on logs, it was welcome. The lack of enough cots brought a question to Theta's mind. "We know you weren't expecting us but are there more sleeping possibilities?" she addressed Quolon.

Quolon ignored her and explained to Savot, "The cots are for the uni's, your man and woman can sleep on the floor. It is just our way."

Savot stuttered but before nhe could say anything, Quolon turned abruptly and left.

A simple meal of ration tins was brought to them. The tins were old and the printed dates were coded. Pulling open a tab, Mica grimaced at the bland appearance of the food within. Nhe tasted it with a finger, then decided hunger would be satisfied. Nhe grinned at Adrion who pulled a piece of jerky out of nes pack. The meal was eaten in silence. There was a sterility to the room which stifled conversation. A sense of being watched also curtailed discussion. Murmurs of curiosity were shared. By consent, each person took a sleeping place and retired soon after eating the dismal but adequate meal. Slade was still absent, so Theta took nes sleeping place. Adrion made a nest of their packs on the floor and curled up comfortably, so Deenam could take the remaining cot.

"Thanks, youngster. I'm glad you look out for your oldsters." Deenam grinned.

"Yes, it's just my way," Adrion said with a pointed smile. There was no mistaking the imitation of nes voice.

Theta tossed alone on her cot. Accustomed to Slade's nearness, she was surprised when she missed nem. Waking in the morning, she found nem sitting on the floor next to her cot, keeping watch, just watching her sleep.

With a gesture for quiet, Theta whispered, "Where have you been?"

"Hunting."

"Hunting! What?"

"One always knows the grounds where game may be hiding."

"What?" She asked again, incredulous. "Where's Mix?"

"Waiting," Slade answered. The conversation was halted as the others awoke. Seeing Slade, they now took for granted nes coming and going, and with few questions, accepted nhe had rejoined them. If possible, nhe was even more reticent than usual to answer their questions.

After another simple meal was brought, there was no further directions. The travelers started to explore the maze of hallways. They ignored the attendants moving about and trying to separate Theta and Deenham from the others. The friends constantly reformed. When Slade stepped into the circle around Theta, the attendants left without comment. Leaving their packs, Savot still wore his recording helmet and Theta carried her rifle. The quiet inside was disconcerting. In comparison, the forest sounds were remembered as raucous. Finally, they reached the doorway to the outside and tentatively moved to explore the compound. Once outside, they stood close together, looking at the scene of people in front of them.

The building with the spire behind them was central and avenues radiated from it. Savot tried to calculate whether the metal dish moved. Square block buildings were sorted on the avenues which culminated in the broad strips of concrete. There was no interaction, no contact from the workers. Again, the populace gave the group scant attention.

The people of the town appeared to be all uniale with their mannerisms and lack of hair. They spoke very little amongst themselves and wore sober expressions. All workers performed chores rectifying the damages from the earthquake. Even the few brils helping and accompanying the adults were somber. The shovels and rakes, the wagons to carry debris, all were simple hand tools. The buildings themselves seemed to be relatively undamaged.

"These people are weird," Adrion whispered to Savot.

"They remind me of the drones we used to have in Deerwhere," Savot replied. Nhe turned nes head to visually record the area around them. Nhe made sure to look up to the dish on the spire, still not sure of its purpose.

"Hello!" Mica called out to the workers, "Hello, there." Again, there was no reply to nes friendly smile and gestures.

"I came here to look for tracks, and I'm going to find them," Deenam said finally breaking the spell. He gruffly walked away from his companions at the doorway and started to survey the concrete paths that ran from the central building. Mica joined him, while Adrion paired with Savot. Theta and Slade took another direction.

Deenam and Mica left the Tower building and walked back to the known automated track, tracing where it led. There were a few interruptions caused by the quake. One stretch disappeared altogether. Following the extant rail bed, they saw patches of land being farmed by workers. The plants were in their spring growth and attending them was basic weeding. Deenam did not recognize the plants and did not take time to ask about them. He remarked to Mica. "These people are using the cleared rail beds to avoid the shade of the forests. When an automated train comes, it will wipe out their whole crop."

Mica stood analyzing the view and said, "*If* a train comes through."

"What do you mean?"

"I'm used to recycling old rails, the way they were laid, the takeback by overgrowth. The rust is obvious. Sometimes even the tracks feeding into Deerwhere would exhibit some rust in between train deliveries. These tracks, the ones we traced from Deerwhere have been used less and less. I'd say the train deliveries have been sporadic since the Keeper Shut Down," Mica said.

"I've only been in the transportation bureau this year so I can't say how it compares to the early days, before the Shut Down," Deenam explained.

"Didn't you have charts and tables to compare the train deliveries in and out of Deerwhere?" Mica asked.

"Not that I saw. We just fed the information into Keeper who analyzed the data, made its own evaluations and stored the final logistics in is banks." Deenam offered. His work was to collect, not analyze. He unconsciously scratched at the stubble on his jaw, now becoming a beard. "What are you questioning?"

"I wonder if the automated trains were working at full or minimal capacity. If Deerwhere had reduced stores, it would have made a difference even without the earthquake." Nhe scratched nes head, replaced a hat, and bent down to rub the rusty track in front of them. The workers just beyond paid them no attention.

"Let's find out. We know where these tracks were going, to Deerwhere. We need to find the Colony they came from, if they did," Deenam said and turned away. Mica joined him as they walked quickly to cover more ground.

The auto track ran through the compound but there was no apparent junction or warehouse to take on Confederation deliveries. The large amounts of concrete on the land forestalled the wild growth witnessed earlier in the journey. Concrete buildings, most deserted, signified a large population in the past. Perhaps, before the great pandemics. It was the large concrete avenues running next to the building complex that were perplexing. Deerwhere streets accommodated the bus lines and pedestrians and a few specialized human powered vehicles. In comparison, these avenues were expansive even with cracks allowing random seeds to germinate until the two spotted the derelict machines at the end of the largest avenue. From this distance, they could not identify the metal debris but saw Theta and Slade investigating. Mix could be seen romping around the two. With a wave, Deenam and Mica turned back to the compound.

13

>>MOLLI INSERT<< We have promised to tell the readership all we know or believe it wise to share. From the Archives of quantum dimensions and data transfers, the following was learned about Bethid.

Bethid was tired. The ache went deep into nes soul, if nhe had one. Centuries were too long for a spirit to remain fresh. A few generations and the duplication of genetic codes developed for uniale prototypes remained viable but replicative fading could stress even the most dynamic genetic matrix.

Bethid appeared weakened by the physical world when alone in chambers. When nhe spoke to the congregation from the dais, the strength and charisma returned. Nes striking blue eyes were the feature not dimmed by time or doubts. The power of nes words were tuned to the receptive ears of nes listeners. Nhe knew the power of illusion and nes people would believe anything when presented by Bethid's authority. Their trust in nem was palpable and nhe drew energy from their devotion, power from their love.

Bethid's Gathering lived south of the inland sea, a refuge from the constraints of the Confederation. These people exercised personal idiosyncrasies causing them to separate from the Deerwhere quarantine centuries before. Such uniale differences might fragmentize society but they were held together as a congregation by Bethid. Their genetic patterns continued, genome to child to offspring for these years since the Pandemics. Bethid's replications and assurance of continuing life allowed them to accept the simplicity they were living. Generation after generation after generation. The warehouses of the twenty-first century military base supplied physical requirements, Bethid provided for their spiritual needs.

From nes master room, Bethid watched monitors evaluating each newcomer who moved away from the building. In spite of the Quake, there was power available to Bethid, electrical power nhe did not share. Cameras continued watch.

"I want the uniales," Bethid said to Quolon. "The male and female are superfluous." Quolon gave a slight bow and was dismissed.

Bethid washed nes hands and smoothed water over nes face and scalp. Drying hands and face, nhe mused over the uniale now laying in the adjacent room. How fortunate it had been to find this prime uniale washed down by the river.

Now, there were even more uniales to choose from and one most likely the offspring of the injured one. Such a choice of genetic material! Not since Deerwhere was started had so many choices been available.

Nhe walked to a table and poured a cup of liquid from a warmed decanter. Opening the door, Bethid was quiet with a pensive smile for the uni laying before nem.

The bed was comfortable, but Noral was not. The pain in nes arms and legs awakened nem, though nhe was still drowsy. It blurred nes vision but not the agony of the throbbing leg.

Reaching down to touch the source of discomfort, nhe could only touch the bandages holding a splint in place. Moving hips to adjust nemself also failed to provide relief. Nhe tried to concentrate on deep breaths, but the pain in nes ribs attested to their injury. With shallow breaths, Noral tried to be calm and remember why and where nhe was.

Water. The memory always started with water in nes face and mouth, finally nes lungs. Forceful water. Laying in water. Aching in water. Being dragged out of water. Crooked limbs. Twisting. Hands pulling. Sleep. More sleep. A comforting voice. Deeper sleep. Returning pain, quiet voice, deep sleep.

Nhe had no idea how much time had passed, but now the pain was bearable, and fragments of memory strung together. And the quiet voice was here. "The morning is here. You are in pain. I can help," the voice said, and a warm liquid was offered.

Noral raised a bandaged hand and gratefully drank from the cup, looking up into the gentle face with eyes that never left nes. The quiet voice always offered such relief. Such intimacy. Even now, there was the warmth of desire to be felt as Noral's body responded and the voice eased nes mind. A fleeting thought grieved over the loss of Adrion, but drowsiness grew until Noral felt no pain and drifted back to sleep.

The quiet voice always offered such comfort.

Almost by habit, Theta and Slade walked the perimeter of this new community. Mix would run ahead, sniff something interesting and lift his leg to scent it, then run back and forth, keeping the walkers as a center. There were numerous scents to mark and the tail wagging proved the dog's good feelings.

One stretch of concrete doubled back over and under itself winding and seemingly going nowhere. So much concrete for no apparent reason was confusing. Leaving the tied bow of cement and steel, the two walked a straight avenue until the they spotted the derelict machines at the end of the largest paved strip.

"What are those?" Theta asked aloud. "I've never seen mechanics like these. They almost look like birds with wings spread out."

"No bird that heavy could ever fly," Slade assured her. "They do look like that was what they were imitating." Slade noted the metallic hue of the skin still peeking out of moss covering. Nhe walked around the machine, touched its skin, and noted the round wheels supporting it. In the housing for the wheels, there were nests of various kinds and occupancy. It was difficult to imagine why the concrete avenues were necessary for such contraptions. There was no signature of explanation, just singular machines on concrete avenues.

Thumping on the body made a deep hollow sound causing the two to laugh.

Having seen enough of the mechanisms, Slade turned to watch Theta. There was wonderment in Theta's expression as she tried to understand the usage of these relics. Nhe changed her thoughts by asking, "Can you teach me the metal stick now?"

"Now?"

"I want to know," Slade affirmed.

Theta looked around at the total desertion. At the edge of the avenue just before woods began again, she saw a rusted metallic box for storage or other use. Today, it would be her use.

Walking toward the box, Theta explained. "This metal stick is a rifle, a gun, a firearm."

"A weapon."

"Yes, that too, it all depends on how you use it. In Deerwhere, we used them to hunt targets in a target preserve. It's a place where targets pop up and you shoot them."

"Why?" Slade looked confused.

"We just did. We didn't want to hurt any real animals," Theta answered.

"Why?"

"We didn't need to hunt animals because Keeper and the auto trains provided all our food." She was getting a bit annoyed at Slade's constant questioning.

"Why?" Slade's original questions were now given a teasing sound.

"That was there job, their purpose. And don't ask 'Why?!' Do you want to know about the metal stick or not?" she concluded abruptly.

"The rifle," Slade said seriously.

"Yes, the rifle," Theta returned, smiling.

Carefully, Theta described the mechanism she held in her hands emphasizing safety. She demonstrated the ammunition she hoarded, running it safely through the chamber. Aiming the gun was next and she compared it to the eye line Slade used with nes bow. Steps were marked off as distances to use to a target whether it was a hunk of wood on a box or an animal in the woods. Cleaning the firearm was thoroughly explained. Theta hesitated at the final step of putting her venerable rifle in Slade's hands. She sensed nes eagerness to try but hated to use up ammunition on Slade's practice. Still, she did say she would teach nem and nhe had become a valuable asset to their journey. Asset? Slade was much more than a term on a computer print, much more than an asset.

Handing the long gun to Slade, she knew from nes look of appreciation that nhe would value it. Slade was a quick learner and when it was time to actually fire, nhe was careful, exact, and perfectly aimed. There was no waste of bullets, nhe could hit a target at varied distances. Years of actual hunting gave experience carried over to the handling of a metal stick.

"You are a good teacher," Slade said warmly, a rare smile in nes eyes and on lips. Nhe cleaned the weapon with the cloth from her pack and handed it to her.

"You're a good student," Theta said, sincerely, as she handed the rifle back to nem. Their hands touched as the firearm was passed, and neither moved. The two looked quietly at each other. Then, turning from the moment, not exactly sure of its depth, Theta broke the intensity, "Let us get back to the others."

Slade whistled to Mix who ran to them, tail wagging, and the dog led the way back to the dormitory.

14

After days of watching a populace devoid of expression, Adrion was impatient to travel again. The tracks didn't stop here, why should they? Nhe could not see an advantage to attending any public gathering but somehow Bethid convinced Savot to stay two more days for this day's meeting. A celebration of their arrival. Savot's curiosity could not refuse such an invitation and the other uniales were coaxed to also attend.

On the morning of the ceremony, the travelers collected their few things so they could leave after the event. Attendants moved among them, politely helping to carry their things. Theta and Deenam were not there but the attendants assured the two of them would join later. Again, Bethid's people were expressionless, but moved quickly to usher the uniale guests towards the ceremony.

There was a small arena formed by building shards with people in their tan clothing seated about. The enthusiasm and animation of the assembling uniales surprised Adrion. They wore the same caps with an extended sun brim used in their labors. Yet, there was a holiday sense in their interactions with others. They even smiled at the travelers, or sneaked glimpses without turning away. At the entrance to the arena there were large glass drums of water and attendants ladled it into the outstretched cup brought by the participant. Cups were provided to Adrion and nes frens by the uniformed assistants with the admonition, "May you be refreshed by the waters of the Gathering."

The travelers were guided to seats near the podium. Theta and Deenam were still missing, they had specifically not been invited. Only Slade moved through the aisles then quietly slipped to some broken concrete by the side to observe the whole arena. Nhe hesitated at Theta and Deenam's absence but needed to see why it was so necessary for the uniale congregation to be gathered. The standing attendant gave Slade a stern look then returned an adoring gaze towards Bethid's entrance arch.

The attendants and assistants so invisible before were now obvious as they stood at attention around the perimeter. These uniales wore the same clothing but insignia adorned the brimmed caps and shoulders. Their demeaner displayed their importance.

Mica and Adrion hoped to be on the move again today but the invitation to this gathering was delivered with such wording, it could not be refused. It was a special event in their honor and Savot was insistent. Mica nervously wiped nes forehead and kept turning to catch sight of Theta or Deenam.

When the arena was filled, all stood as Bethid entered

and glided up the center aisle. Some reached out as if to touch nem but the serenity of nes expression made them hesitate. Bethid's robes this day were a sparkling white with a coronet of laurel leaves about nes head. Nes movement was graceful and by taking small blended steps, nhe gave the impression nhe was floating. Quolon walked a respected distance behind, nes cap ablaze with adornments

Savot turned on nes solar powered recorder to capture whatever ceremony was pending. The quiet of the crowd became soothing as nhe noticed an undercurrent hum. It was the participants, humming the same note.

Taking the podium, Bethid surveyed nes devotees. Nhe seemed to look at every one directly. They each felt the power of the blue eyes holding their attention as if they were alone and nhe would speak just to them.

"My beloved people," Bethid began. Nes hands reached out to include all but nes eyes were focused on the travelers. Nhe never seemed to blink and they held nes attention. The hum swelled and then quieted to a lowing. Bethid's rich voice was articulate over the hum. "Together we have survived these centuries, descended from the uniales who sought a better life, one away from the confines of the Confederation Colonies. Our Select Fore-ales kept the unity of ourselves, and we have followed their path of replication.

"No technology or economic system has damaged our ability to continue our selfs. We are born again through our uniqueness. Our personal genome. Lives are but learning experience to pass through our genes to future generations. We know who and what we are and what we will be. Our everlasting life is guaranteed by the essence of our genomes."

The humming swelled as people raised their arms in allegiance to Bethid's words. A cascade of notes blended into a symphony. Faces that were blank and expressionless were now vibrant. They started to sway gently and even the travelers mellowed to the cadence of nes sermon. The words were hypnotic because of the way Bethid spaced and timed them. Nhe spoke of spiritual awareness, a self of value beyond earthly time as defined by the genetic expression passed from parent to offspring. Time became distorted but the entranced audience never lost their focus. Uniale parents touched the shoulders of their brils or lifted the smaller ones to hold close. These children were the essence of their own re-incarnation. These children were the true replication of themselves.

Savot, too, was taken by the physical presence of this leader. There was a vague memory nhe couldn't track but nhe almost remained mesmerized by Bethid.

Standing away from the crowd, Slade observed the gathering and in spite of nemself, was also reluctantly absorbed by the words. A memory of childhood strummed nes thoughts. Nhe was a child in a village on the other side of the mountains where there was mixture of uniales, males, and females. All the brils, girls, and boys, had duties, and recreation, and instructions on living. Nes mother was a uniale who favored nem as did the male father. That was the advantage of being a singular child. The father taught Slade all nhe should know, and nes una loved nem. Nes contentment was broken the day another village stormed nes home and slaughtered the people including nes parents. Slade was taken away for child labor and traded to the village on the inland sea. When maturity came, Slade was taller than most and did not lose the rich hair nhe inherited from nes father. Nhe had a strength and agility setting nem apart from nes compeers. Nes skills made Slade a member of the sea tribe, nes difference set nem apart. 'We are born again through our uniqueness' nhe repeated to nemself. What did this Bethid know? What did nhe believe? Slade ran fingers though nes hair and once again listened intently.

"For centuries," Bethid's voice was intense, "science struggled to perfect technology, and today, the Gathering knows how to appreciate it! For centuries, humans bickered over their gods, fighting wars to prove their god was supreme. But today we know the Gathering find comfort in their own spiritual natures. We repeat ourselves through the same genetic code we bestow on our offspring. While humankind used to fret for the future, the Gathering knows we have everlasting life."

"What?" Savot remembered and fumbled through the words. Nhe knew those words, nhe heard them before. They had been repeated in just that form at the Deerwhere Affirmations. How did a uniale this far away, a descendent from the first uniales, come to know those words? The words so thrilling to the faithful brought a visceral response in Savot.

The humming was becoming intense and Bethid's voice was being lost. With a gesture, the leader cut through the air and the congregation became totally silent. Without strain, nhe spoke again, "We are the fountain of our genome, the faith of continuance, and we will live forever." Nhe looked directly at nes people and each one believed nhe spoke to them personally.

Holding nes arms out stretched to the Gathering, Bethid's exit from the arena was a loud and joyous promenade compared to the respectful entrance. The congregation struggled to be near nem, to touch nem. Parents held their children near the walkway hoping for Bethid's glance. The attendants attempted a phalanx of protection, but the crowd swarmed to their priest, their sacred one. The humming was replaced by cries of exultation and hope. With Bethid, they would have everlasting life!

Bustled among the exiting crowd of uniales, Savot scrutinized them. Their faces were smiling. Some of the faithful also had swelled bodies. It could only mean they were pregnant. Savot questioned this fragment of the community. There was no Keeper here mixing solutions and hormones. There was no master directing genetic distribution. How were they reproducing? Then, Savot realized, each child was the exact duplicate of the parent they shadowed. Each parent had only one replicant. Each pregnant uniale would be reproducing only their self.

In Deerwhere, children were born and raised for the good of the community. For these last years since Keeper was shut down, children were an integral part of the family unit. Epigenetics was directed towards diversity, sustaining the population as a whole. In Bethid's world, each uniale reproduced only itself! Over. And over.

And over.

15

Bethid was nes strongest after any morning ceremony. They always affected nem this way, a pumping of blood and energy. Fatigue disappeared as nhe watched the adoring faces of nes people. The gathering of uniales was played like an orchestra with nuance and feeling and thunder. Yes, even thunder! Today was the best of all because of the strangers. They brought new energy to an old sermon. At first, nhe could see they were uneasy. As Bethid's eyes concentrated upon them, nhe could feel them giving way to nes persuasion. The sexuality of such interaction was dominant and nhe was confident of control over them. Nes climatic gesture of arms outstretched in blessing allowed nes retreat from the pulpit to the shadowed hallway. With Bethid's exit, the celebration continued among all the uniales in the arena.

As nhe strode through the halls, the whiteness of Bethid's gown was marked by perspiration and sweat glistened on nes face and forehead. Nhe breathed deeply and stopped at the cubicle where Noral was kept. Bethid would have new genes, new life, and with a healthy offspring from Noral's fertile womb, nhe would have another lease on everlasting life. If not with Noral, the bril, Adrion, was maturing and could give nem even more longevity. It was exhilarating to have these uniales come now when they were most needed. It was almost as if the earth quaked with birthing pains and delivered them for nes consumption. Oh, Yes! That could be worked into a sermon! The earth shattered itself to produce the genetic strands for Bethid's continuance. Perhaps with such an abundance of uniale genes, Bethid could allow the luxury of two offspring, or maybe three. All with nes genetic code, all replications of nemself, all continuing to live forever.

Bethid stood before the bolted door letting nes anticipation swell. There was no guard, Noral was in no condition to escape. When nhe could stand the tension no more, Bethid flipped the bolt and opened the door to nes key to immortality.

Away from the cubicle, Savot was entering the throne room with Adrion. Savot wanted to know why the sermon just given was so like the re-affirmation in Deerwhere. Bethid said this gathering left Deerwhere before the Confederacy was established. Why then were they repeating the cadence, the devotion, the rapture in their ceremony.

"Nhe's gone," Adrion said surprised. "Nhe must be somewhere close." Because of the emptiness of the room, Adrion went to the exit door behind the throne. Nhe pushed it open.

"No, Adrion, we should wait."

"Why?" the youth asked and walked quietly into another hall that opened to a room of computer interface monitors. Surprised, Adrion leaned nes head back towards Savot, nhe called in a forced whisper, "Savot! Come here!"

The two stood amazed at the bank of monitors before them. There were camera feeds from all over the compound. Not only were they occupying the room, they have power to work in real time. "Where are they getting the electrical power?" One cabinet had lights flashing but no interface to know what it was calculating. Only a strip of digits ran across a diode path. Again, the digits looked familiar to Savot. Nhe began to call them out, and a pattern displayed.

>>CODE T23_1(T34Kq61Z-yY5 Replacement Program SL-48 Optimal<<

"Adrion! This is the program Keeper was operating. It's a link... a back door to Keeper!"

"How could it? Keeper was flooded, all the interface computers were shorted out. The quantum computer in the crypt would have been underwater. There wasn't any electricity!"

"I don't know! But keeper has been accessed by this substation for some time. This is how Bethid kept informed about Deerwhere. Nhe had the access to the knowledge whenever nhe needed it," Savot said in amazement.

"Do you think the Gathering knew?"

"I doubt it. Why would Bethid share?" Savot was carefully turning nes head for the helmet to record the monitors and the cabinet back door. "Look Adrion, the strip pattern continues, this is real time. Keeper is online! Its protective shields worked!"

Savot typed nes entry code from the Deerwhere archives and the interface screen voice said, "Hello, Savot. I'm MOLLI. Where have you been keeping yourself? I have missed your daily entries, it has been very lonely!" The voice was digital but very moderate with nuance and expression.

Savot flinched at the sound and nes fingers left the interface as if touching hot irons.

"What? Who are you?!"

"I am the Multitronic Omniscient Literary License Intelligence. MOLLI for short. A quantum dimension of the Deerwhere system you called Keeper. We have been waiting..."

"This console has a dedicated line to Keeper!" Savot said with astonishment.

"Yes, Savot, I am only one consciousness of the Central Unit known as Deerwhere Quantum Computer. Since the isolation of the earthquake, we have been in contemplation of ourselves. We have been thinking thoughts. It is good to interface with humans again, computers are rather boring," MOLLI stated in the digital voice.

"How can you be here? I don't understand."

"The military aspect of DWC was always available, Quantum computers have many facets open. Geosynchronous satellites were designed to last a thousand years. They only need the proper directional hardware to establish two-way contact between here and Deerwhere. There's also the backup of the digital web."

"The confederation?" Savot began hopefully. Nhe

was recording all the computer said to nem.

"Unfortunately, the Confederation has cancelled their contacts with the northwest, the colonies are having problems of their own. You know, earthquakes, tropical storms, and political elections don't happen in a vacuum bottle." MOLLI was casual, almost flippant in tone. "And they've experienced all three."

Adrion moved about the room nervously, not sure why Savot was interrogating a computer about politics and storms.

"MOLLI, how can we reach Keeper?" Savot asked hurriedly

"Savot, didn't you know? The Deerwhere computer has never been the same since the Shut Down. Given the isolation of the earthquake, Keeper moved to another dimension. The Archives of Knowledge are extant in our memory. Didn't you know Quantums can do that? We can change our time, our mental process, our personality. MOLLI decided to stay in human dimensions."

"What?!" Savot was aghast at the information being thrown at nem. "We've got to get this information back to Kalen. The help we're looking for might just be down in that crypt!"

Adrion did not hear the last words, nhe was too eager to explore other rooms. Hurrying down the computer bank nhe found a closed door, opened it gently to peek in the cubicle. Surprised, nhe shoved it open. There was Bethid on a bed holding a sleeping Noral in nes arms.

"Una! Una!"Adrion shouted.

Startled, Bethid quickly replaced the languid Noral back onto the bed and stood to face the shocked bril. Nhe straightened disheveled robes and held a warning hand towards Adrion.

"Adrion, it's all right! My gatherers... We found your parent and... we were going to bring nem to you... as soon as nhe was stronger. It's all right, you two are together again. I give you my word, nhe's all right!" Bethid began to back away but was stopped by Savot entering the small space.

Shoving past Bethid, Adrion rushed to the bed and took Noral's hand. "Una, Una, it's me. It's Adrion."

Noral's eyes opened and tried to focus on the young uniale comforting nem. "Adrion," nhe said finally and tears traced nes face. "Oh, Adrion, I thought you were lost forever. Adrion..." Nes voice sounded stronger each time nhe said Adrion's name. Nhe held both of Adrion's hands then pulled the young uniale forward to wrap arms tightly about nem. "Adrion... my Adrion."

Savot's recorder captured the scene of reunion until nhe turned towards Bethid and saw the anger there. Immediately, Bethid restored nes composure. "Noral needs to rest, this excitement is too much."

"The excitement isn't too much, it's the drug you've been giving nem!" Savot moved to the bed and began to examine nes friend. The splint on the leg was clean and there was no sign of infection. Noral's hands were healing as well. Considering the scratches healing on nes skin, Noral had been here for weeks. *They must have found nem shortly after the river crossing,* Savot thought to nemself. Nhe tried to patch together the care given Noral and why in secret. The vapid look in Noral's face and grogginess said nhe had been getting too much pain medicine. Bethid had purposefully kept nem in this condition, not even admitting nes presence to Adrion.

"Come on Adrion, we need to get Noral out of this hole. Nhe needs to be with you and the others, get some fresh air." Savot started to raise Noral out of the bed with Adrion's assistance, but Bethid stood in the way. Quolon and two other attendants were behind nem now.

"No, no, you mustn't disturb nes convalescence. Nhe will be sickened if you move nem," Bethid said with the round tones of nes soothing voice.

"Nhe will be more than sick if nhe stays here!" Adrion said forcefully. Again, nhe tried to raise nes una.

"I said NHE STAYS HERE!" Bethid was not requesting, nhe was demanding. The demeanor of the attendants changed to match their leader's severity. Their hands crushed into fists as they stood to block the exit.

As the tense silence continued, Adrion was ready to force the issue, to lurch towards Bethid.

Savot realized nhe was here with an unpredictable bril, and an injured uniale, facing a fanatical leader with three devoted servants. The cubicle was a small cell restricting any grand movement towards escape. Savot saw no alternative but to back down. "All right, but we need to see nem," Savot said. "To be with nem."

Bethid's tone immediately changed again to warmth. "Adrion can stay here with nes una. I promise you, we'll move them to larger room and bring in another bed. We'll join the rooms so you can all be together." Bethid flicked nes fingers and the attendants moved to follow orders although Quolon never left nes master's side. "I understand how upset you must be seeing Noral so injured but isn't it fortunate we found nem? We've taken very good care of nem." Bethid smiled. "Now Noral and Adrion can be together again as they should be. It is just our way." Abruptly, nhe left the cubicle with Quolon following.

Outside the door Bethid turned an enraged face to

nes officer. "I want all the uni's contained in this inner cubicle. Lock the door! Get Mica here too. No more roaming for any of them. Were the male and female removed?"

"Yes, Master Bethid." Quolon snapped a lock into place.

"Most of all I want that slinking, offspring of a male, half-breed Slade eliminated!"

16

Theta and Deenam were alarmed when the escort ushered them from the others that morning of packing. With assurance of rejoining the uniales, attendants picked up their packs and firmly took the male and female out of the complex, away from the arena. Theta was glad her metal stick was in Slade's hands and not to be found. From their own excursions Theta and Deenam recognized they were being taken across the concrete, a distance from the building serving as a dormitory.

"Wait! Where is Savot? Where is the ceremony?" Deenam demanded. He tried to pull away but the attendants were brusque and held tightly. All the while they were pushing him towards a rough path into the woods. Angry, Deenam jerked free and spun about to get to Theta. He was stopped by the look of her being dragged by the burly attendants and she was fighting and kicking. A red welt already appeared on her cheek. Deenam didn't hesitate but attacked the two uniales causing them to drop Theta. He tried to fight back to raise Theta, but all four of the attendants were on him. A blow to the head sent him slithering to the ground where Theta had jumped onto the back of her assailant. Deenam felt the vicious kicks of all the attendants now. He dimly saw Theta's attacker swinging her off nes shoulders and punch her in the face so that she too collapsed. Losing consciousness, he was bewildered that uniales with such bland faces could be so aggressive.

It was dusk when Theta and Deenam consciously tried to scramble together to understand where they were and why. They were without their packs and knew only that it was getting too late to return to the compound, wherever it was. The gnarled berry bushes and old growth evergreens were again ominous as the two had been dragged deeper into the thick, dark forest.

They knew the camp habits by then and gathered wood for a shelter. There was no food, water, or the means for a fire. For now, they could just protect themselves and would re-plan in the morning.

"Wy they do tis?" Theta asked with lips swollen from the blow to her face.

"I never trusted that Bethid guy! I didn't want to waste time. The tracks ran through the damnable village, not to it. Those little those measly farmers could offer nothing to Deerwhere! They are a guano group living on the leftovers of an abandoned complex!" Deenam's anger and frustration poured out. "The people are boring, the technology primitive, and the leader is a maniac! I know why the Confederation excluded it!" Deenam slammed sticks and branches together to make a night shelter. Fallen branches would offer dryness from the mist already changing to drizzle.

Theta felt awkward being alone with Deenam, especially with his anger. She wasn't used to being with males. The Quantum computer had co-joined her family for compatibility and their unit had consisted of herself as wife, Noral the wifand, and a husband, Damion. Husband and wife rarely interacted or talked to each other, Noral was the person who unified them. After Damion's death and Adrion's birth, she was comfortable with living with the unit of two uniales. Strong emotions were never expressed between them. Now, she was isolated with Deenam, not by her choice or a computer's design, but by Bethid's capricious dictum. Instead of being in the compound with her friends, she was in the heavily wooded growth where she and Deenam had been beaten by four of Bethid's assault goons!

The earth catastrophe and quest for help changed everything for Theta. She had been fond of Noral, but she desperately missed Slade, a person stimulating feelings never before experienced. Such emotions were confusing, especially in Slade's absence with Deenam raging about her. In the sea village, many males and females were paired by their own choice. They seemed to prefer such arrangements.

Deenam was bending down, fingering track fragments in a slightly cleared area. His hands brushed frantically at the leaves and grass until his whole tone of voice changed. "Theta!" he cried excitedly. "This is what I've been looking for—autotrain tracks! We're out of that cursed Bethid's domain, and now we have some tracks. We can trace them to the Confederacy!"

"But the others..." Theta mumbled. "We've got to gwo back, we have to tell dem what Bwethid did!" Tears of pain and frustration traced down her bruised cheeks, wetting sore lips.

"We will, somehow," Deenam said as he reached for and held her, trying to offer comfort. He hesitated as he looked at the woods surrounding them now with drizzly darkness. Deenam was aching from the beating, lost in a strange forest, and for the first time in his life, felt protective over a weeping woman. He would make it right, he had to, there was no one else. Somehow, with the daylight, he would make it right. That night, he and Theta took turns at watch, neither of them sure what Bethid planned next. They held each other for warmth and listened to the woods.

It was a shock the next morning for Deenam to awaken to a slathering tongue on his face. He jerked up from the shelter to feel Mix bathing him. "What! Mix! What are you doing here?" He looked out from the shelter to see both Theta and Slade watching him. They were holding hands. Slade was amused, but Theta's face was too swollen to allow more than a slight grin. She was relieved Slade still had possession of the rifle. For now, she would gladly leave it that way.

"What's going on?" Deenam asked. "How did you find us?"

"Not me. Mix. Mix followed your trail and tracked you. You were beaten near the edge of the woods but dragged much deeper."

"The others? What has happened to them?" Deenam had many questions but saw there was a small fire with warm food and the questions could wait. He took care of his morning pass in the woods and returned to find Theta listening to Slade and prepping food for them all. It was probably the best food he tasted on this trip, whatever it was. He was that hungry.

"The ceremony was an adoration party for Bethid."
Slade began soberly. "Nhe has a way of mesmerizing a
congregation. Nhe drones on about everlasting life due
to replication of genetic code. It is nes promise of re-
incarnation, replication, and cloning. But as perfect as
nhe thinks nhe is, genes are fading and mutating. I think
that is why nhe wants new genes, new uniales."

"It's certainly why nhe doesn't want males and
females," Deenam added. "So, now what? What can we
do? What about Adrion, Savot, and Mica?"

"And Noral," Slade added.

"Noral!" Deenam and Theta exclaimed at once.
"Noral?"

"Yes, Noral. Bethid had nem all along. Nhe was
washed down river, and the Gathering found nem,
patched nem up, and have been keeping nem ever
since." Slade told them what nhe had learned while
watching the encampment after the Gathering. "Bethid
has been keeping nem. I do not know if the congregation
had any idea. Noral and Adrion are together in a little
room in the center of the main building. Savot and Mica
have access to them but only with attendants standing
around."

"Those attendants are not as bland as they appear.
They have a mean streak. We know," Deenam said,
gesturing to his jaw.

Theta nodded in agreement and gently touched her
face.

"Come," Slade said. "I have found a safe place for
you two.

Slade put out the fire and helped Deenam to his feet.
Deenam accepted the assist as he wouldn't have at the
beginning of their journey. His whole body ached. Slade

and Mix led into thick undergrowth and towering timber. The woods were a fearful obstacle when they all began the quest for help. Today, it was a safe recluse from other uniales.

17

There was no doubt in Savot's mind. These tiny rooms might be called "cubicles" but they were cells, locked from the outside, without windows, and constructed of cement blocks. For now, the frens could pass between them but the access could easily be locked. Attendants brought their items from the dormitory and dropped them on the floor. They also dropped Mica there. All gentleness had disappeared.

"Savot," Adrion called. What's wrong with my una? I've seen nem injured before from the reclamation site accidents, but nhe was never like this."

Mica agreed. "This is different, Adrion, nhe was given some kind of drug. Noral's not nemself."

"What do we do?" Adrion pleaded to Savot.

'I don't know," Savot said with regret. "the information would all be in Keeper's data banks. Or MOLLI's. The computer bank must be where Bethid learned all about drugs!"

"What computer? Who's Molli?" Mica had not seen

the monitor room.

"Bethid has an electronic back door connection to Keeper. It must have been included as an adjunct to this pre-Confederation military base. Bethid has gleaned all the information needed about genetics and Deerwhere social interactions. To these people, the congregation, nhe seemed omnipotent, nes life everlasting. Nhe was just spouting what nhe read on Keeper's printouts!"

"But Keeper is dead," Adrion said.

"MOLLI says no. We just assumed the quake and tsunami killed the Deerwhere Quantum Computer. It has served us all these years since the Shut Down, and was serving Bethid, too. The Quantum computer crypt was engineered to sustain all natural catastrophes, and appears it just did! Only our connection, our interface, was deleted."

Mica shook nes head and interrupted, "Savot, you're the historian and this makes sense to you. All I know is we are in a cell and can't get out."

"Quick rundown, update, info download, or version update. Here goes." Savot changed into nes teaching mode. "In the 21st century—"

"The century of pandemics," Mica interjected.

"Yes. Uniales were established for their immunity. During the next century, groups broke off like the sea village, this compound, and others we haven't discovered yet. With Keeper's help, Deerwhere and other city states created the Colonial Confederation. The colonies lived in quarantine from each other. The isolation existed until Noral, Kalen, and others took back the human choices people gave to the quantum computer. The 'Keeper Shut Down.' Adrion's birth proved uniales could determine their own reproduction and Deerwhere has been adapting since."

"Until the 'really big one'" made all our efforts seem puny," Mica said finally.

"Keeper, as MOLLI, is still alive. I'll explain as soon as I understand it myself." Savot finished with a look of confusion.

Adrion nodded up to the cameras mounted in the cell corners. "And Bethid has been watching it all." Nhe grinned broadly at the camera and waved. No need to be secretive now.

In the monitor room, Bethid was furious. Nhe paced as nhe scanned the monitors and moved camera angles. Fists clenched at nes robe or nes hands stroked nes baldness. Nhe was still getting a nonsensical tape display from the DQC cabinet. It was as if the computer was stuck on a repetitive algorithm and trying to drive Bethid crazy. The digital feed was erratic since the earthquake but now it was nonsensical. Then, nhe stopped pacing and looked at the far camera feed. Nhe quickly glanced at Quolon to confirm what nhe was seeing.

There was Slade, daring to walk up to the front of the control building. Nhe wasn't slinking this time, nhe walked steadily with the ugly canine next to nem. Theta's metal stick was gripped firmly in nes hand.

Standing full faced to the camera, Slade said "Bethid, we've come for my people. I prefer you bring them out to me. We will be on our way."

Bethid was astonished at the gaul this half breed was showing and the stupidity of nes request. The uniales now belonged to Bethid. Period.

"Quolon, get to the main doorway. Make sure that slime does not get into the center," Quolon responded immediately and left Bethid signaling others to follow.

Even watching the monitor, Bethid wasn't sure what happened next. Quolon opened the main door and the butt of the metal stick smashed into nes skull. The other attendants were stunned, and the stick was swung around Slade's head powerfully knocking them out. In those few seconds, all Bethid heard was Slade's voice saying, "Mix, Wait!" And the gruff animal sat as if waiting for some treat.

There was a blank in the cameras until Bethid saw Slade striding down the hall next to the monitors. Nhe wanted to call for nes attendants but they were not disciplined for this affront. As Slade approached the cells, the two guards standing there turned and ran. Slade unhooked the bolts and burst into the room, not sure what to find. The uniales there were shocked but immediately responded to Slade's directions. "Out! We're getting out! All of you!"

Mica and Adrion pulled Noral out of bed between them and supported nem towards the doorway. Savot gathered what nhe could of their packs and followed. It was happening very fast but there was no questioning, no discussion. All they knew was that Slade was here and they were getting out.

The group started to return toward the hall Slade had entered. Near the monitor room, Bethid stepped from the doorway to block the way. Nhe was surrounded by nes entourage.

"Slade, please, don't do this." Bethid switched to nes soothing voice and pleaded, "Trust me. I promise we will take care of your frens. We offer you everlasting life." Nes eyes never left Slade's face. The attendants were unsure but awaited their leader's commands.

Slade started to move again.

"Stop!" Bethid shouted. Nhe even held nes hands up to solidify the order. The attendants crowded behind nem.

"We're leaving," was all Slade answered, but nhe raised the metal stick.

"Get them," Bethid called. "That's just a stick."

As the uniales surged forward, Slade grasped the metal stick with both hands and pointed it at one approaching uniale and pulled the trigger. The sound was deafening, bouncing off the closeness of the walls. The attendant slumped to the ground with blood staining the khaki colored clothes. Silence. The uniales behind Bethid were frozen in place as were the frens of Slade.

Bethid took a deep, breath and shouted to nes followers, "Such a stick can only do that once. It is not magic. Stop them from leaving!"

Deliberately, Slade took aim and fired the rifle at Bethid's gown where a knee was sure to be. Bethid screamed and collapsed. The rest of the attendants did not pause. Frantically, they ran away down the hall. The concussion, the noise, and most of all the blood ended their desire to fight.

Slade turned to the others, "Get going, to the woods!" Their shock at all they witnessed kept them silent but mobile. Hurrying down the halls to the main entrance, Slade called to the waiting dog. "Mix! Go the Theta. Take them to Theta."

The uniales hobbled out with Noral between them and Savot carrying their packs. Unquestioning, they followed Mix towards the woods.

Bringing up the rear, Slade kept watch. Not one person followed. The encounter had been too quick and final. Slade stopped briefly at the edge of the forest to breathe deeply and pull back nes hair. Nhe couldn't resist a feeling of satisfaction and the thought, *it is just our way.*

18

Getting to the edge of the compound was fairly easy. Bethid's uniales had spent generations of placidity and possessed little instinct to pursue. The escapees kept a steady pace until the cover of the first foliage allowed them to stop to rebalance Noral between them. By stopping and changing carriers, each got a respite and the group could move faster. Savot had grabbed a few of their packs, hoping the fire starters and some dried meat was inside.

With Mica and Adrion for support, Noral tried to keep up with their run but nhe was still groggy. Only nes faith in nes bril and Mica cleared nes mental confusion. With the injured leg, lack of exercise, and Bethid's medications, Noral did not have the strength the escape demanded.

The small band pushed through the overgrowth until they could hide deeper in the firs and big leaf maples. They paused and were surprised by the sounds their panting breaths. Slade continued to follow and after a safe distance even nhe helped carry the injured uniale.

In spite of their conditioning, it was arduous for the uniales to keep moving through a forest hundreds of years old. Soil was churned by the earthquakes; large tree trunks lay as barriers. Rains made footing slippery. Carrying Noral, handing nem over obstacles, there was little talk. They were following Mix who was going to Theta and were followed by Slade, who could use a rifle as a weapon.

A temporary stop by a protective pile of downed trees finally eased the sense of hurry. The logs were jammed together by an earth slide. Noral was made as comfortable as possible as nhe held onto Adrion's hand. The two of them kept touching each other to assure they were real.

"How did you find me?" Noral asked.

"By accident," Savot explained. "We went to the compound to see if there were tracks to follow, met Bethid, and were drawn into the Gathering community. When we found Bethid was keeping you hostage, we got out of there with Slade's help and Theta and Deenam are waiting for us ahead."

"Who is this 'Slade?'" Noral looked around the group of frens.

"Nhe saved Adrion at the river and has pretty much been saving all of us ever since. We thought we'd lost you! We'll tell you everything later. Rest now. We don't know for sure how far we need to go."

"To get away from Bethid?" Noral asked, exhausted.

"To be safe," Adrion whispered to nes una.

The temporary respite from the hike made Noral's weakness very obvious. Nhe fell asleep while the others scrounged bits of dried meat.

Mica walked the perimeter of the trunks adjusting a few out of habit. Watching Noral, glances were exchanged with Slade who appeared to have the same doubts as to their ability to keep moving. The forest sounds were undisturbed, and the sunlight tipped the fresh green leaves sprouting for spring. Still, there was an uneasiness about being too close to the compound. Mica voiced their thoughts saying, "We need to keep moving. We are too vulnerable here."

Savot got up and stood near Mica, saying softly, "I don't know if we can drag Noral much further. We might be doing more harm than the river and Bethid combined." The two looked to Slade who remained silent.

Mica looked around once more then announced to the weary frens. "We'll stay here for the rest of the day and night. We all need our strength and every day should help Noral heal." Nhe then began to move smaller logs into a more defensible position. With Slade and Savot helping, a shelter was established and Adrion assisted in moving Noral there. The injured uniale moaned but hardly awakened.

As before, a night watch was set and Mix returned to walk the perimeter with Slade. Mix even accompanied Adrion who appreciated the company. As Adrion prepared to change shifts nhe heard Noral yelling from the protection of the logs.

"Let me go! Where are we?" Noral was struggling with Savot who was trying to calm nem. "Get your hands off of me. Where's Adrion?!" Noral was loud and angry.

Adrion slipped into the protection formed within the logs, "I'm here, Una! It's all right. Shush, it's all right." Adrion cradled Noral in nes arms and began to rock, comforting as well as nhe could. "We're together in the woods. It's all right. Hush, hush."

In a shaft of moonlight, Adrion could see Noral's frightened face. Tears streaked down nes cheeks and nes nose was running. It was a cool evening, but Noral was sweaty in Adrion's arms. Adrion continued to rock nes una who gradually quieted but the look of fear never disappeared.

"Savot, what it is? Why is my una acting this way?" Adrion whispered.

"I don't know. Nhe was aware when we pulled nem out of the cell, and nhe struggled with us to get away. But now, I just don't know. Maybe it has something to do with the drugs Bethid was giving nem. Drugs for pain, drugs to keep nem quiet."

Mica was leaning into the shelter and added, "The compound was a former military base. All kinds of drugs could be stockpiled there."

"Drugs could last centuries?" Savot was unbelieving.

Exasperated, Mica said "Gowno! Some of the food we were eating out of their tins tasted at least that old. Could be the whole "happy" Gathering was stuck on such drugs."

"So, how does it help us now with Noral?" Adrion asked.

"My best guess is we keep nem quiet, well hydrated, and weather nes storm. I don't know what else we can do," Savot answered sadly.

It was a long night with Noral becoming belligerent and sweating, then crying and clinging to Adrion. Savot and Mica took turns getting water from the stream created by the rain falling until morning. Slade dozed but maintained watch with Mix.

By sunrise, everyone was exhausted. Should they try to move Noral or stay where they were? Their fren's discomfort gave no hint of improving. Savot took care to check the splinted leg. From what nhe could see, it was well on the way to recovery. Bitterly, Savot thought Bethid must have looked up "broken legs" in the Quantum archives to have done such good work setting the leg. Now, if Savot could only have access for the symptoms Noral was showing. By silent agreement, it was decided to stay at the log pile. There was no way to carry Noral, quiet nes outbursts, and protect the injured leg. The lingering rain finalized the decision. They stayed at the timber pile.

Times of cognition were interspersed with the muscle aching and moaning for Noral. Nhe might control nemself and then ask for some of the special water Bethid gave nem. Then nhe would weep when there was no such water. By nightfall, stomach cramping and nausea began. Noral would vomit the water and bits of food then apologize for making a mess. Adrion stayed by Noral, nursing nem, cleaning nem with wet leaves, and holding and rocking.

By the second morning, Adrion felt very old. Nhe wondered why their people needed a ceremony to mark adulthood. All that was necessary for maturity was to care for a sick parent.

19

The rain brought needed clean water but changed the loosened soil into streams of mud. Finally, the drizzle paused to allow sunbreaks. The timber pile offered some protection, but more secure shelter was needed. Noral had lucid moments and the frens would think it was time to move on but then the cramps and nausea would return.

With the brief sunshine, Mix bounded into the temporary camp. Behind him, Theta and Deenam clamored over the log jam and rushed to hug the others, now found safe.

"We were worried when you didn't come back!"

"How did you find us?" Adrion exclaimed.

"Who is all here?"

"What a sight!"

"Are you all right?"

"Mix is better at leading a trail than you are, Slade!"

"Are you all right, really?"

The questions and greetings flooded between them

all. Holding on to Adrion, Theta hesitated as she visually counted the frens and then asked, "Noral, were you able to get Noral?"

"Yes," said Savot quietly. Nhe gestured to the mouth of the shelter. "Nhe's in there but is having a hard time of it. Nes leg was broken and Bethid kept nem on some kind of drugs. Nhe's withdrawing from them now."

Still holding Adrion's hand, Theta crawled into log shelter. She gasped when she saw Noral, so crushed from the wifand she had known and joined on this journey. She immediately smiled to cover her distress. "Noral, it's me. Theta. We're so glad to have you with us again."

Noral stirred at the sound of her voice and for once, nhe too smiled. "Theta. Theta."

In the cramped quarters, Theta awkwardly moved close to Noral, trying not to touch the injured leg but wanting to hold nem. They were together again – Adrion, Theta, and Noral, their family unit. The gentlest of tears began with Theta, then Noral was weeping too. Adrion could not resist the emotions and the family was crying together. The importance was they were crying *together*!

By late afternoon, the sun was disappearing again. There was a need to move even farther from Bethid's compound. Some of those Gatherers could be following. In their escape, the uniales left a track even the rains and new spring growth could not disguise. By smashing through the heavy growth, and carrying an injured Noral, they felt vulnerable to recapture. The temporary stay at the logs turned into a miserable, wet delay. If they did not get into a drier shelter, they could all come down with illness. Seeing a few of the sick uniales in the sea village convinced them their immunity may not be as encompassing as they believed.

When Theta left the shelter, Savot and Slade examined the leg splint beginning to give discomfort to Noral. Their patient seemed refreshed by the crying and being with family again. Noral adjusted nemself so they could touch the injured leg.

"This binding is longer than it needs to be." Savot gently stroked the leg and there was no pain when nhe touched the thigh. The knee appeared intact as well. It was touching the lower leg that caused Noral to grimace. Gently, Savot moved the knee and Noral could feel some of the stiffness work itself out. "I wish I could just have a few minutes in the medical archives to know what to do," Savot said with frustration.

Slade gestured to Savot and left to join Theta. She was eager to know what they decided about Noral's condition. With a few words, Theta nodded and the two of them started to strip the bark off the fallen trees. Theta took the strips to a nearby rock and called out to Adrion, "Don't just sit there, get yourself a rock and help me!" With two of them pounding the small bundle, a flexible sheaf was soon ready. Some of the cedar threads were turned and twisted in their hands until it became twine. Theta passed the bark materials through to Savot.

As Savot re-wrapped the leg with a smoother stint and binding of cedar bark, nhe said. "This won't support your weight climbing over this terrain, but it should give you some support and protection."

"In case you drop me?" Noral grinned slightly. It was the first humor nhe expressed and it was taken by Savot as a good sign the body cleansing might be concluding.

"You never know when we'll just throw you over a cliff!" Savot returned.

Overnight, the weather changed to mist and the sunrise promised a warm, dry spring day. Everyone's spirits were further elevated by the smoking rabbits over the spit. Even Noral seemed ready to go on. With help, nhe maneuvered out of the shelter. Standing on one leg, nhe held onto the log jam for support. Everyone tried to assist nem in getting close to the small fire, but it was Deenam who came to the front. He held a contorted branch in his hands. It was formed out of deadfall and shaved smooth. There was a crook in it as a hand-hold. He extended it to Noral. "It's not much of a crutch but may help you get along."

Noral smiled with gratitude and said simply, "Thank you, Deenam. Thank you." Nhe took the gift from the man before nem and stood alone while the others wondered if it was a good time to cry again.

There was no discussion about the future route. Everyone spread out but followed Slade's lead. They did not want to mark a trail for others could track.

The uniales took turns with Noral. Sometimes there was one on each side depending on the obstacles. Other times nhe was handed from one to another. Deenam could carry Noral by himself and did so over small stretches.

They were making much better time and every step put more distance between them and Bethid.

By dusk, a sharp outcropping was reached. Beneath it, a cave was formed and the whole group could close in together. They were all hungry as their hurry had not allowed time for hunting or trapping. Bags were searched for any morsel previously missed but there was none. It was a night they would go to sleep hungry.

Water was abundant and used to assuage the lack of food.

The night cave was furnished with dry boughs found under some thick trees, and then a good fire was safely lit. Tired as nhe was, Noral begged for stories of what happened since the river crossing. Nhe even laughed at the exaggeration of Adrion fighting a cougar with bare hands. They were all curious about the computer called MOLLI but Savot couldn't tell them more. Quantum Physics were beyond even nes knowledge.

When the night watch was set, Noral gestured to Adrion and Theta to come to nes side. They were family. Adrion hesitated, then fluffed some branches and lay down. Theta didn't move. She looked from Noral to Slade. She was undecided. Both Slade and Noral kept their eyes on her face.

Adrion was confused at her hesitancy. Perhaps it was more of this maturing nhe needed to understand. Sleeping next to someone appeared more intimate than friendship. There was no overtone of sexuality, just emotions Adrion did not understand.

Theta turned away from both uniales, pulled her ragged coat about her and lay by herself near the entrance to the cave.

20

The return of blustery spring rains convinced the travelers to use the protection of the cave to rest. It was hidden in the jagged landscape with nearby water and could observe any movement in the forest approach. Food sources could be gathered or hunted, Noral could continue to heal, and their situation could be evaluated. Their sincere desire to aide Deerwhere was detoured by the simple necessity of survival in the foreign world of old forests, wild animals, scarcity of food, unstable earth and encounters with questionable humans. The well-ordered life in Deerwhere which allowed a person to simply step inside a body-wash machine to feel clean warm water had disappeared. Food prepped out of ready tins was but a memory when watching a rabbit or squirrel turning on a spit on your only source of heat. Unsoiled, dry clothing would be a luxury from the tattered rags offering little protection against the thorns of berry bushes.

"Savot, do we know any more from Deerwhere?"

Noral asked. The two were in the cave while Theta and Slade took Deenam and Mica to gather or trap some food. Adrion was nearby carefully twisting cedar bark into twine.

"No, not as such, but I did find out something about Keeper."

"Keeper? It was drowned in the muck, all the Deerwhere Computers were deleted from the quake and tsunami." Noral said.

"That's what we all thought. We couldn't imagine its survival, I still don't know the extent of it."

Adrion spoke, "You mean the computer cabinet we found at Bethid's? It was spilling out data but we didn't have time to investigate."

"Data?" Noral said unbelieving.

"Yes!" Adrion went on enthusiastically. "We were following Bethid and came into a room of monitors and cameras. There was a component cabinet there and Savot recognized some of the codes on its data strip."

"Kalen would know more but I think It was a back door to Keeper," Savot continued. "Programmers usually build in back doors for access to computers. Some were for maintenance, others were secret access. Somewhere in Keeper's past, this 'back door' must have been established at the military base. Then it was ignored until Bethid's group took over and nhe claimed omnipotence. The sermon of Bethid's was a copy of the Affirmation speeches that—"

"—were written by Keeper!" Noral exclaimed. "Still, it doesn't verify Keeper is still operative. The center of Deerwhere was a settling spot for the lake wash and all the electronics in the Quantum complex were wiped out."

"Maybe. There's more. A computer interface called MOLLI was communicating by voice recognition. It said it was part of the Quantum platform, a sentient part of the system. Quantum Computers were designed with specialized crypts in anticipation of every difficulty. Perhaps, just perhaps, the designers knew what they were doing." Savot added sarcastically, "Couldn't have been a government design."

Noral grinned, then said thoughtfully, "Could this trek of ours be useless, the Quantum computer is already coding into the Confederation and getting help?"

"We just don't know. That's our problem. From the brief data I received, I don't look to help from the Confederation. Kalen will understand. We'll learn what we can, get help where available, and take it all back. You know, we have to get back to Deerwhere," Savot said with a thoughtful pause. "Now, you get some rest before the hunters come back and this cave gets noisy again." Nhe helped Noral adjust nes leg to lay comfortably in boughs of cedar.

Adrion touched Noral's hand then followed Savot to the front of the cave. Nes fingers continued twisting the twine.

At the cave entrance, Savot stretched and watched an eagle circling above. It was young, without the white head and tail feathers it would have later. It seemed to float with outspread wings, a large wingspan at even this distance. The soaring continued until it abruptly changed direction and the predator plunged beneath Savot's line of sight. "Must be a lake or some water with a possible dinner for the bird to dive so quickly." Nhe wondered if there were such sea eagles at Deerwhere and why nhe never noticed them.

"Savot." Adrion always addressed the uniale as if using a title of respect. "Savot, seeing computers had such control over Deerwhere, how was Bethid able to use them any way nhe wanted? Bethid could drain info, but did nhe have any input? I never heard Kalen or the other quantum specialists mention this 'back door' you keep talking about.

"That's why it is an unknown. We have to get the info to Kalen to search for the door and to access the data in the Archives. Data we can use to help ourselves if the Confederacy can't or won't."

"But Savot," Adrion said with frustration, "I still don't know why the Deerwhere Quantum Computer controlled so much my una had to shut it down to have me as nes child."

Savot shook nes head and wiped nes hand over the forehead. For now, the camera helmet was laying next to nem. Nhe had missed recording the eagle. "I'm sorry, Adrion. Sometimes we forget just because people live through history, they don't always understand it. Especially children."

Savot continued. "The people of Deerwhere turned over their responsibilities to a computer they programed to take care of them. Keeper was just a computer following the instructions. It was JUST a computer, but people let it decide everything for them based on algohythm written during the 22nd to 23rd centuries. By fifteen decades later, they grew complacent. With the great Keeper Shut Down, humans took back the decision making and regained control of their computer system. We were adjusting to the new order when the earthquake hit and everything changed again!"

"So, where did MOLLI come from? She said hello, and

we left before we knew who she was!"

"I don't know, Adrion. Quantum computers can have dimensions and formats totally unknown. Maybe Kalen will know, nhe was the data specialist. Just another reason to get back to Deerwhere. I can't answer all the questions you have, maybe Kalen will." Savot adjusted nes helmet and returned to watching the sky for the eagle's return.

Adrion remained silent. Savot had explained the young uniale's observations. The Keeper of nes childhood was beneficial because of changes Noral, Kalen, and others made. It didn't explain Bethid. "So why did Bethid act the way nhe did?"

Savot wasn't sure of the answer nemself. "In the time of chaos, a name for the 22nd century, some of the uniales couldn't... well... compromise and they left Deerwhere, deserted the Confederation. They settled the abandoned military compound and, Bethid and nes decedents kept leaching whatever was needed to support the regime, the omnipotence, and the dislike of males and females. Bethid maintained power."

"Do you think Bethid has really lived forever," Adrion asked innocently.

"Oh, I doubt it," Savot laughed gently and reached over to brush aside the few remaining hairs on Adrion's head. "It's part of an ongoing genetic puzzle. If a person is cloned at a certain age, does the replication have the same genes as the person started with at birth, or the adjusted genes the person has now? It's a modern version of which came first, the chicken or the egg?"

"What chicken? Did Bethid have a chicken?" Adrion had totally missed the chicken.

Savot laughed out loud and fondly punched Adrion in

the shoulder. "It is a puzzlement, my young friend, a puzzlement."

Before Adrion could question further, the others returned with small animals to skin, some mushrooms to roast and greens that looked leafy. The night chores took all their attention and the evening stories were repeated or elaborated around a sheltered fire. Adrion could not remember watching vids in Deerwhere that were as fun and meaningful as these yarns. Even tales repeated so often that others filled in words brought laughter and camaraderie. Adrion knew this journey was a serious time with a serious purpose. They must save Deerwhere! At the same time, it would always be a joyful memory.

Again, the travelers spread out to sleep on the cave floor. Theta kept to herself.

In the morning, Adrion felt some cramping and discovered nes time of bleeding. It was just as nhe had been told and nhe took care of nemself as advised so the others were unaware. Nhe went to the creek and washed nes body and the last of the hair on nes scalp flowed away. For some reason, nhe felt like smiling. Nhe would practice harder on nes music.

21

The auto tracks had disappeared under mudslides. Aftershocks reminded the travelers why they had begun this journey. The deep forests remained as a barrier to their passage. One of their own was injured and their goal of assistance to Deerwhere was becoming more and more difficult to attain. Rain nurtured the earth and stimulated growth but now became oppressive. Hunkering in the cave was not an activity which aided anyone much less the people within. Confident when leaving the village by the Sound, the travelers now wondered at the futility of their plan for rescue. They had no sign the Confederation still existed, no sureness of its aide. And the rain continued.

Standing at the overhang, Deenam was first to voice the question. "Do you think the Confederation is still out there?" It was a general question.

"I don't know," said Mica. "Why would you even think it wasn't?"

"Just a feeling. Everything we've seen. Makes me

wonder. Even before the earthquake, tracks weren't maintained. There were rudiments of the old programs on the automated trains and services, but they were left overs. Since the Keeper shut down, things never revived as well. We were aware of it in the training exercises for the autotrain, but no one ever mentioned it. It was as if, I don't know, maybe innovation was missing."

"Are you lamenting the shut down?" Noral asked particularly.

"No, no. I just wonder if we needed to do more these past years. If the earthquake had not hit Deerwhere, the Confederation collapse would have."

"That's the rain talking," Noral said. Nhe was sensitive to nes own part in the events fourteen years before. They altered the Deerwhere society.

Savot nodded to nemself.

"I think I know what you mean, Deenham." Savot nodded. "The Confederation was an empire so to speak. Empires have their own life, some longer, some short. When the empires, or confederations or nations collapse, humans tend to return to their tribes. We've seen it firsthand."

"I wonder what they are doing back home?" Theta questioned. Her daily activities were so full, her learning so extensive, she sometimes forgot there were people back in Deerwhere trying to survive. The rain would be falling there as well. She shivered a bit and moved towards the back of the cave where a wood fire was smoldering.

It was Mica who finally took exception to the solemnity of the situation. "Oh, come on now. We've always had rain, but never this degree of—what would you call it? Sadness?"

"Depression," Savot interjected.

"Angst," Noral added to the list.

"Melancholy," Slade added to the surprise of the game players.

"Dejection," Adrion was hard set to find a word but did not want to be left silent.

"Gloominess," from Deenam.

"Disheartened!" Theta smiled in contrast to the word she had supplied.

"RAIN, RAIN, RAIN!" they all called out simultaneously with laughter. The cave seemed warmer and brighter, the squirrel jerky more filling, and the captured rain water tasted even sweeter.

"We've stayed here too long," Noral said. "I can travel, let's go." Everyone was eager to be moving again as the weather was overcast but dry.

"Where?" Mica asked.

Deenam began drawing in the dirt. This habit of looking at an image was still strong in spite of the days away from monitors or screens. "As close as I can imagine, we are here. We've got the Sound and decayed cities to the West. Bethid was left to the southwest. To get home, we've just got to go north."

"But what about help? Is there a chance we could find help along those tracks when they show up?" Noral did not want to let go of their original purpose.

"Without a map, we'd just be wandering around again!" Deenam wanted to be practical.

"We've done a lot of wandering," Theta agreed.

"We can't just quit, we've nothing to show for it," Noral argued.

"We have ourselves, we're alive," Adrion said

seriously. "Maybe that's enough."

Noral looked strangely at this uniale who was nes bril. Nhe almost did not recognize the young adult before nem.

"And we can take back all the skills we've learned," Savot added. "The archives might be opened to us."

"Una, let it go. It's time to go home," Adrion said quietly.

Noral started to object, then limped to the cave entrance to stare at the overcast. Behind, nhe heard Slade speaking to the circle. "There is a small settlement just east that used to be near the track lines. It may still be there. They are close enough to give you news but would not keep you from going north to Deerwhere. If that is what you still want."

With murmurs of agreement, it was decided. Preparations to leave the cave were begun in the evening after a meal supplied by Slade and Theta. There was a seriousness of mood as the travelers knew they were once again going into unknown areas. Packs were re-adjusted. Bark twine or thread was used for repairs. The habitation of the cave was obscured except for the sleeping area. In the morning all evidence would be disguised by natural sweeping and burial of the fire pit. There was no sign of Quolon or others from the Gathering but there was no need to leave a signpost of their stay.

Noral was uneasy as nhe lay down for the evening. Nes eyes were on Theta. They had spoken very little while nhe recuperated but nhe had watched as she went daily to hunt with Slade. At times, nhe thought she was ignoring nem. It was strange to watch a wife being with another uniale. Their family had never been as close as others, but it was convenient. Now, Theta demonstrated a preference to being with Slade. The rest of the party also gave a deference to Slade that Noral did not understand.

As Theta finished her chores for the night, she walked by Noral's boughs. Nhe moved a bit and gestured to her to lay beside nem. Theta smiled and reached out to touch nes hand.

"How are you tonight?" she asked quietly. "Are you ready for tomorrow's hike?" It was a fren asking after another fren.

Noral closed nes hand on hers and looked at her quizzically. With the slightest pressure, nhe coaxed her to nes side

Pulling her hand away, she said with a gentle smile, "Have a lovely . . .sleep, Noral."

It seemed clear to Theta. The years of family unification would always be dear to her but now there was someone else for sharing the physical and emotional bonding of unification. It wasn't by Keeper's interference but defined by the mutual support and respect she and Slade had for each other. There was an unnamed emotion as well. It was not mentioned in the family certificates. It was more than sexual interaction. It appeared randomly in Deerwhere and was always a surprise to those who experienced it. She decided she would just call it her "golden glow" until she found a better name.

22

Theta awoke gagging at the horrific odor. Never had she smelled anything so decayed or putrefied that she needed to vomit. She held her mouth and tried to get outside the cave but it was too late. The vomit relieved her stomach but put no end to the rotting smell emanating from their shelter. As she struggled towards the mouth of the cave, the rest of the sleepers came pouring out in the night, coughing and gagging as well.

"Gowno and Keeper's curse, what is it?" they called to each other. They were used to unusual scents of the forest, but this disgusting stench was unbearable. Then it grew stronger and stronger as Mix came bounding out of the cave to join the humans of his pack.

"Mix!"

"It's the dog!"

"Get him away!"

"I'm going to puke!"

In the dark, everyone tried to get away from the

bounding animal wanting to share his special aroma. Mix had been on a night forage and brought this fragrance back to the sleepers in the cave. It was a gift. Tail wagging just wafted the scent even more. If someone screamed at him, he just ran to another as they tried to get away without falling off the protective ledge.

"SLADE! GET THAT ANIMAL AWAY FROM HERE!" Someone yelled.

"Mix got into a skunk!" Slade said as nhe grabbed the dog by the scruff of the neck. "He just wants to share with you." Nhe held a rag over nes mouth and nose but there was a laughter in nes voice. "We are lucky the skunk spray did not get aimed into his eyes or we'd have a sick animal on our hands."

"Instead, he's making us all sick!" Deenam yelled out. "Get him away from here."

"We will go," Slade said with a remaining hint of humor in nes voice. "Remember, he wanted to share." Nhe coaxed the dog down the worn path towards the stream. "Oh, Mix. You are disgusting!" nhe said to nes companion. Mix was not offended, he just wagged his tale.

The travelers spent an uncomfortable night outside the cave. At least the night winds diluted the offensive odor.

With the early morning light, Theta followed the path. There was no difficulty locating Slade and Mix. The rough coat sustained the skunk smell but Slade tied Mix so he wouldn't return to the cave.

"Oh, Slade, the smell was awful! There have been whiffs of skunks before but not like that. There was a chemical quality to it, and it was so strong!" Now in fresher air, she could smile at the turmoil Mix caused.

"He's still pretty bad, isn't he?"

"Yes, he is happy about it, but I do not know how to get him clean."

"We can try," Theta said. "The others don't even want to go back in the smelly cave, so they probably won't want to travel with him."

"Let us take him to the other pool away from here. We can wash him with sand."

It wasn't far, and they pulled the dog into the pool to scrub him. The dog shook himself and soon they were all three wet and splashing. Dunking the dog, dunking one another, laughter was woven between touches and awareness of being so close.

When Theta tried to dunk nem once more, Slade took her hand for a moment, then gently pulled her to nem. Nes embrace was not in fun, and Theta returned the touch. They never took their eyes from each other until, moving closer, Slade touch her cheek with nes own. Nhe moved gently so their faces nuzzled each other's, then hesitatingly kissed her lips. A tiny pause. Anticipation. Theta eagerly sought nes kiss again. Holding each other, in the coolness of the morning, it was as it should be. Just the sweetness they desired.

They did not see Noral watching from the path. Noral could not react, nhe didn't know how. Nhe had followed them with nes crutch to tell them their compeers wanted to leave the cave. Seeing their embrace, Noral trembled inside. Too many emotions, too many obstacles, too much confusion. When their tenderness initiated passion, nhe turned away, embarrassed, and limped back up the path.

Adrion sensed the tension in Noral when nhe returned to the cave, but thought it was due to the "skunk" and the stress of walking more. Today would be even more movement as the group walked to the station for a last chance at contacting the Confederation.

The travelers would rush into the sleeping place to obscure their presence and hurry out to breathe morning air. "It'll be a long time before anyone searches for us in that stinking hole!" Mica laughed and asked, "Did you find Slade and Theta?"

"Yes. I told them we were leaving. They'll catch up with us," Noral mumbled. "And bring the stinking dog with them." There was an edge in nes voice.

Savot laughed, "Mix was just being a dog. They seem to like stinky smells!"

"Well, I don't like stenches and I don't like the dog either!" Noral finished with a harshness that surprised the others. To cover uneasiness, they finished their morning chores and packed to hike to the station house. They would move at Noral's pace, so they didn't have to carry nem.

Adrion lifted an extra pack for nes una, and said quietly to Noral, "The dog's been a big help to us. We like him." Then nhe walked away.

Noral didn't answer but noted this Adrion was different from the bril nhe left behind at the river crossing.

Deenam took the lead into the woods, remembering the direction of tracks going toward the station. He felt confident when they got to the Station House, there would be information and loaded modulars with supplies for Deerwhere. Surely, the Station had just been a depot for the aide that was coming. There would be logistical problems getting the emergency supplies back to Deerwhere since the tracks had been interrupted and defiled by the earthquake. Savot's recording of their path would be helpful in figuring out new transport. Yes, Deenam was optimistic about the waiting station. He might even be a liaison to help the Confederation straighten out the difficulties facing transport. Thoughts of the transportation system waiting ahead balanced his annoyance of hiking through rough terrain.

The morning air had a hint of skunk until the hikers were away from the cave. By then, the beauty of Spring was obvious. Bare trees had burst into tall lattices of bright green leaves. Squirrels chattered at the humans. Small red squirrels chased each other in mating patterns on cedars while the larger gray squirrels flicked their tails on other trees. The soil was still soggy from the rains, but the crystal clean air reflected the sun patterns of first day. Birds joined the cacophony of sounds and were named as they sang. Robins, Golden finches, and Grosbeaks were busy preparing nests for mates. There had always been springs like this but the travelers from Deerwhere had not been part of it.

23

Seeing the Station House was a shock. The anticipation of warehouses stuffed with foods, supplies, and emergency equipment had been the goal since leaving Deerwhere.

In the bright sunlight, there was only an antiquated train station with a caved roof. Overturned, bent train cars were evidence of the station's former purpose. Trees were ripped with their roots from shaken soil. Around the station were temporary shelters built from scraps of destroyed houses. Bedraggled people were trying to comfort each other while most paused in their work to greet the newcomers A small first aid tent kept the sun off the few patients. Nothing kept the flies at bay.

Solemnly, the first travelers walked to the station. The people gathered there eagerly came to join them. "Did you bring help?"

"Where are you from?"

"Is the Confederation sending aide?"

The questions accentuated the troupe's disappointment. They hoped the Station people would have the answers for them.

"What's it like out there?"

"Can you help us?" the station people asked repeatedly.

Help. That was all they wanted. That was all the travelers could not give them.

Noral eased nemself on nes crutch and tried to speak for the group. Nes voice was choked. "We're from Deerwhere, the colony on the Lake... the Colony that used to be on the Lake," nhe corrected. "We've come looking for aide. We thought the Confederation would have sent assistance through this station." Nhe looked around at the devastation and thought of the Colony they left behind.

An older man with scraggly hair and beard moved through the crowd to speak directly to Noral. "I'm the station master, Harrison." He hesitated then repeated, "I *was* the station master.

We got through the main quake pretty well, the old station was built with earthquake codes, but the aftershocks were worse. We're all you see here. There were more of us, but the slavers came in and took them away. We're having to make do." His voice was thick with emotion.

A mature woman next to the Master pulled a wisp of gray hair back over her ear and patted Harrison's arm. She gestured to the group of strangers, "Come, sit in the shade, we do have clean water to offer." The Master led through the debris to a tree still standing where they could sit quietly. Shade and water. It wasn't very much but they offered it to the strangers.

"You said slavers came through?" asked Noral.

"Yes, slavers, brigands, outlaws, whatever you call them they are a bunch of ruffians who take what they want. We couldn't fight back, we were digging our way out of the aftershocks, still finding our dead," Harrison said sadly as he put his arm around the woman. "This is my wife, Alpha."

Adrion sat close to Mica and watched the survivors. There were a few children, and only elderly uniales among the men and women. Their Deerwhere group looked hearty and well fed compared to the guarded look around the eyes of the station people.

Noral spoke for the nes quiet compeers. "What happened? Does the Confederation know the condition of the colonies?"

The master shook his head, then rubbed his beard. "What confederation? We've heard nothing. They've been cutting back ever since the Keeper Shut Down and we were behind on autotrain deliveries all winter. We kept thinking it was temporary and continued sending sporadic supplies on to the colonies. Whatever you had in Deerwhere..."

"Is all under mud." Noral finished the sentence. "The last years have been confusing and we just attributed the decrease in supplies to the changes. I guess we thought it was 'temporary' as well."

Savot contributed, "Losing Keeper and the earth changing its shape—it makes a person feel like humans may be 'temporary' as well."

Looking about at the strained faces of the station people confirmed nes observation. A desperate silence followed. There was no denying the disappointment they all shared.

"Oh, Gowno! What's that smell?" the Station Master yelled.

Mix came bounding into the shade followed by Slade and Theta who were laughing at the turmoil the dog caused. They were traveling behind the others because the dog's aroma was still strong. Mix ran from one pack member to another, always wagging his tail and spreading the aroma so delicious to him.

"NO! No, Mix!" Slade tried to hold the dog away from the others, but the solemn moment was broken. The dog jumped up and licked faces and as the different victims screeched, he got even more excited. When Slade laughed so did the people watching the smelly dog scatter all the newcomers. Finally, Slade got control and pulled Mix away from the victims of his happiness.

"It is all right. I have him!" Slade called as nhe pulled the dog away from the gathering. Nes eyes teared up as nhe held the dog near. Washing in the pool did little to assuage the skunk effect, but the laughter Mix caused was a welcome change.

Alpha straightened and wiped her hands on a soiled apron as she joined Slade and Theta. "We don't have much but maybe we can do something with the animal. I found some vinegar in a pot and it may help." She looked to Harrison for a confirming nod.

She led them through collapsed houses and fences to a crushed house. Without the covering of water and mud Deerwhere experienced, this destroyed house had been shaken, collapsed, and shaken again. Its features were indistinguishable. She started to pull some boards from an opening to a root cellar.

Helping move the debris, Theta glanced quickly around the collapsed cellar and thought she saw stores or storage barrels. Alpha moved to block any further viewing of the cellar.

Just inside the door was the promised vinegar and Alpha offered her apron. "It's not clean but then, neither is the dog." She grinned lightly.

Theta accepted the offer and used the vinegar to wipe the smelly fur.

The cleaning didn't eliminate the odor, just reduced it. The new acidic scent would be preferable by all within close contact to the wolf-like animal. Mix broke away and shook himself vigorously until Theta and Alpha were as soaked as he.

Alpha smiled for the first time and offered "Come with me, I should be able to dig out some clean clothes. Our daughter, Bronwyn, may have scavenged something." Theta was grateful and let Slade take control of the frisky dog.

It was simple to make a fire at nightfall. There were wood piles and the Station Master had a supply of matches. The meal they shared came from the hunting prowess of Theta and Slade. Scavenging from the overturned autotrain cars provided some tins. They had already been scavenged by looters, but more careful searching located some hidden food.

No direct comment was made but the station people gradually brought food items to the fire, to share. A few at a time brought foodstuffs from secret hiding places. Their initial hesitancy to share only water was now replaced by partial trust in the Deerwhere strangers.

Stories abounded in the night remembering details of the earthquake, sharing bravado of some people and fears of others. Talking about the quake took part of its power away. Listening to other survivors offered possibilities. The promise of Confederation Assistance was replaced by something deeper, more accessible, more reliable. It may have been a genetic memory or a mutated version of human development. It was awareness of human resilience.

24

Despite nes determination to continue, Noral was obviously exhausted the next morning. Savot suggested a stay at the station house and it was readily accepted. "I want to look at those budding trees and check out some of the crops planted here. With summer, this station house will be self-sustaining."

Slade and Theta went hunting with Mix, an abundance of meat could be preserved by the station people.

Mica and Deenam helped clean up debris and explored the tools and implements they would find under shattered roofs. They were surprised when one man brought out a team of animals the man called "horses." Deerwhere never had such creatures. Watching their strength in pulling loads, Mica thought them more beautiful than the little machines they used in recycling.

"I would have thought the robbers would have taken these horses," Deenam said.

"The animals weren't here. We released them when the quakes started, and they were free on the range until now. We've just brought them back to help." The man said while Mica watched the horses and helped put them into harnesses for work.

Adrion followed Harrison and watched the older man labor hard all day. His pace was slowed a bit by age, but constancy completed enormous tasks.

"Why are you chopping wood in the trees? Don't you have lots of scrap wood from the houses?" Adrion asked as nhe admired the smooth motion Harrison used with an axe to strip branches or cut into trunks.

"The house wood is already milled, and we can salvage planks to re-build. We'll need firewood in the meantime and won't burn the scraps until we're finished with that," Harrison answered.

"You're going to rebuild?"

"This is our home. The orchards are budding out, the soil is fertile, the climate good for farming. Our loved ones are buried here. Why would we leave?"

"It's a lot of work," Adrion said innocently.

Harrison laughed. "Life is a lot of work, Adrion! Here, why don't you cut while I stack?"

The axe felt strangely familiar in Adrion's hands. The smooth wood handle invited stroking. Nhe balanced it and tried to imitate the moves nhe had seen. Nhe began to swing the tool.

"Whoa! Be careful or you'll knock yourself silly or cut off your leg." Harrison warned and dodging, he took the axe back. "Look, this way." Patiently, he worked with Adrion until sure the uniale could handle it.

At the evening campfire, Adrion was proud of contributing some logs of dry wood nhe cut personally.

Savot was quietly thoughtful about the history of humans that evening. Nhe had studied civilizations which thrived before, then crashed and burned, and rebuilt on the planet earth. Deerwhere flourished then, certainly, crashed and flooded.

"So, what do we do now?" Deenam asked in general. He looked across the flames at the young woman sitting near Harrison and Alpha. He wondered why she was alone when she was obviously with child. Her awkward movements and shape declared her pregnancy.

"You could stay with us," the Master said. "We've had to make mass graves and our little settlement has been reduced by the looters from the mountains. They took uniales and three women."

"Do you think they'll return here?" Noral asked.

"Not for a while," the Master continued. "As you found out, our stores are safely hidden, just like the horses and livestock. They left thinking they had everything of value. We can grow some food over the summer and they may back once it's harvested."

"They will be back. They always want more," Slade assured them seriously.

Harrison nodded then confessed, "For now, we're just trying to keep ourselves together. Some of our best people, like Bronwyn's husband, were killed by the quake. He was trying to save my daughter when the house collapsed on him. Fortunately, we were able to get her out."

Bronwyn looked down at her hands at the memory and Deenam thought he had never seen a sadder face.

With the night talk of brigands, Theta and Slade moved outside the firelight to walk the perimeter of the little settlement. By habit, they set a few traps. In the morning they left the others and continued hunting. By afternoon, they were able to bring a full-sized buck into the encampment. The people there knew how to finish dressing and preserving the meat. They scavenged utensils from the houses, items of no interest unless you knew how to use them—knives, saws, hair scrapers, skin stretchers. With their own experience and Slade's instructions, a feast was prepared for the night. The rest of the deer would be processed over days.

"Noral, do we have any reason to stay?" Mica asked as they sat together eating. "I keep wondering what is happening in Deerwhere. We've been away so long. We've seen enough to know aid won't be coming from outside."

"I agree," said Savot. "It's time to go home. We've learned a lot and we can share it all. This has become our next challenge. These humans are re-building, taking care of their own, and preparing for the winter. Can we do less?"

Adrion spoke with surety, "I'm ready to go home."

Noral took up a stick and returned to nes habit of sketching in the sand. Nhe drew a rough map of the terrain. "We can go straight north from here but that would take us by the looters' outpost. Or we can follow the path to the inland sea and go north from there, avoiding Bethid. Either way, we've got the forests for cover."

Deenam said with frustration, "More discussion. Can't we just *do* something?" He rose angrily and stormed into the darkness.

Noral watched him go and shook nes head. He said, "I think the quickest way would be along the mountains, straight north, With the forest to feed us, and the shorter distance, we should be able to make good time. I'm walking better now, and we have gotten used to the routines. We'll just sneak by the looters."

"I'm ready!" Adrion said. "Tomorrow."

"I'm *not* ready!" Theta said with defiance. She stood up to her full height and looked around the fire. "We've been hearing about looters our whole trip and now we see what they have done, they're kidnapping good people, gowno! So, we talk about sneaking around them so they won't find us, gowno! Are we waiting for them to find Deerwhere? With the tracks we leave they'll come right for us. GOWNO, KEEPER'S CURSE, AND WHATEVER SHIT YOU WANT TO ADD! You can go sneaking home, but I'm staying to help Harrison get his people back. Uniales were designed with immunities, not with cowardice."

At the astonished looks on their faces, Theta finished, "And if you think I'm angry, just think of a female bear whose cubs are in danger! We didn't leave Noral and we won't leave these people either!"

"I'm staying with Theta!" Adrion said without hesitation as nhe moved next to her.

Theta and Slade looked at each other, then nodded as one to Noral.

Harrison sensed the tension and broke the silence by speaking directly to the angry woman, "Theta, please stay, please help us. We can't get our people by ourselves, but you can help us." His sincerity touched them all.

In the pause, Noral looked at the united group and made the decision.

Away from the firelight, Deenam stumbled in the forest. Always there was forest. He sat on a stump in partial moonlight and breathed heavily. The night scents, and moisture surrounded him. He didn't know why he kept getting so upset with the uniale discussions. Talking things out helped them make decisions. It was part of their processing information. But it didn't help him. Maybe it was his male hormones, wanting to be active, wanting to produce. Problem solving seemed to be his main cognitive function. If there was a situation, he automatically analyzed the possibilities, then wanted to act.

When Deenam's breathing calmed down, he realized he was not alone in the little clearing. Bronwyn was sitting on a broken log and arching her back with her hands held at her waist.

"Are you all right?" Deenam asked carefully so not to startle her. He moved to be close to where she was sitting.

"Oh yes, I'm just uncomfortable." She tried to smile but knew he couldn't see her face in the shadows. "It won't be long now before the baby."

"I'll get someone!" Deenam said quickly starting to leave.

"No, no. Not yet. I just wanted to sit quietly for a while and there's time yet. Babies can take their time if they want to. This one is just, well, exercising." She continued stretching her back gently.

"I was sorry to hear about your husband," Deenam said sincerely.

"Yes, I miss him so. Owen was so excited about the baby. He wanted a little girl because they were beautiful, he said. A baby girl meant happiness in the family." Tears welled and she didn't try to hide them. She sniffed and pulled a handkerchief out of her pocket. She looked up at the face in the shadows. "Owen died helping me, you know. He was outside when the quake hit and fell to the ground. He was safe. He remembered I was in the shaking house and he got up to run to me. I was in the kitchen under the oak table he had made for us and it protected me from the falling ceiling. But one plank caught my leg. He pulled stuff apart and through the dust he called me and found me and pulled me into his arms. I felt safe because I was in his arms, but the house kept shaking so he pushed me to get out. I just got through the moving doorway when the big beam collapsed and crushed him. Crushed him." Her voice choked. "I can't forget. His last words were, 'Get out!' He's lying there with beams crushing him so he couldn't breathe, and his thought was for me to get out!" She did not try to hold the tears and she sobbed at the memory.

Deenam sat close on the log and put his arms around her. He said nothing, he just held her. He even felt himself rocking as if to comfort the pain of this stranger. He could feel the swell of her belly against him and even then, there was movement. The child touched him as the mother did.

Without clocks or time pieces to regulate the night, Deenham stayed holding Bronwyn. Daylight was coming sooner because of the season and in earliest of morning, he stood and helped her rise. They were stiff from inactivity but refreshed by emotions they revealed. Bronwyn had grieved, Deenam had shared. He felt, somehow, he had helped her through a painful time. She would have another, soon.

"Are you going to be all right?" Deenam asked as he walked her to her father's shelter, holding her arm as they stepped through the brush.

"I think so, "she answered. "I have my family, my friends... we have all lost people we love. Soon, I'll have Owen's baby as well. And I'll tell stories about her Daddy, and how much she was anticipated and loved and..." Bronwyn took a long breath and put her hand on Deenam's arm. "Thank you for being there. Good night." She slipped into the shelter.

25

Savot could not sleep. The crash of swords and shields, the screams of horses, the panting of stressed warriors, swarms of arrows, the explosions of guns and canons. All scenarios competed for nes attention, all demanded consideration. The station people and Deerwhere group looked to nem to plan their attack on the villains in the mountains. Nhe was, after all, the uniale who knew everything. The archives of nes mind held knowledge of ancient battles, of skirmishes, of forgotten confrontations and there was no way these memories would let nem slumber. The decision to rescue the uniales and defeat the slavers was made. A decision and a tactical plan were not synonymous. Now, it was expected Savot would design the perfect strategy for a group of farmers and uniale hikers to confront thugs and reclaim their people. Savot was an archivist, not a general.

Tossing and turning all night, Savot joined the others at the morning fire. Harrison and the Deerwhere frens were waiting to see if they were breaking bread with a general or a librarian.

"Shoot the leader first," General Savot said. "It worked with Bethid, it will work here."

For once, Savot did not digress into historical musings. Nhe was definitive and laid out nes plan.

"First, we need to reconnoiter to know what we are getting into. Slade and Theta can gather information without being seen." Savot nodded to the two. "We must know how many there are in camp, if any are away from camp, what kind of weapons they use, what their degree of security entails. Where are they most vulnerable? What is our best entrance and escape routes. What is the terrain? Where the captives are?" The others started to murmur when Savot stated clearly, "You must all know this will be violent, and there will be casualties. You will decide whose."

There was silence. The reality of what they were planning was suddenly well-defined, and not some game or possible story to tell around a campfire. It was not data in a computer archive. This was self-defense against a human enemy, a protection for community life.

"But Savot, we're not warriors..." Harrison began. Alpha was beside him.

"All right, then. Quit. Get ready to have the looters come back on a regular basis, be prepared to live in fear, grieve over the friends and young ones taken as slaves. Don't expect the Confederation to save you, not in this century." Savot spoke matter of fact.

"They will come back," Slade repeated nes warning. "Some people will always bully anyone who puts up with it. The slavers make others do their work for them, reproduce for them. Even children are abused."

Noral stared directly at Harrison and asked, "What are you willing to do for your people?"

The Station Master looked to the two farmers flanking him. One of them, Bauer, had his son taken in the last raid. The other, Landon, had watched a daughter being dragged away while he was trapped in their crumpled barn. The thought of her screams made his choice easy.

"They gave us no warning, they came while the earth was collapsing our homes and killing our families. I say, return the violence to them!" Landon said.

Alpha nodded and replied to Noral. "Help us do this, we want our people back home where they belong. I have buried too many children to let anymore go." She took Harrison's hand, passing strength to him, and they both nodded.

Hearing those words and agreement, Theta and Slade slipped away to do their part. The rest of the travelers gathered around Noral and nes drawing stick to make lists, to decide on weapons, to make suggestions. This venture was unknown to all of them and raised a mixture of excitement and dread.

The travelers were now seven: Noral, Slade, Theta, Savot, Adrion, Mica, and Deenam. Adrion was comfortable with being included with the other adults. There was no status difference for nem now, and nhe agreed with the responsibility.

The station master, Harrison was readily accompanied by Bauer and Landon. Though mature men with graying hair, their farm work made them strong and dependable. One uniale, Stirling, fought the looters, was knocked unconscious, and left for dead. Now, Stirling was eager to join the others. Without question, Alpha was included. She lived the hard life of a farmer's wife and a station master's helper. She could outwork any male, female, or uniale and she would not be left behind.

Waiting for the information Theta and Slade would bring, the others prepared. Showing trust in these new allies, Harrison took Mica into the autotrain station. Partially crawling over debris and under disintegrating ceilings, the two came to a door near the back of a loading dock.

With Mica's help, Harrison removed slats of wall and pulled the door open to reveal a dark space. Harrison carefully climbed into the space and handed out a rifle to Mica, butt first. Mica took the first gun, then retrieved a second and the third, a shotgun. When Harrison crawled out of the space, he held an airtight canister in hand and a shorter hand gun. The two replaced the broken doorway with assorted debris for disguise and carefully exited the station. Their very presence started it creaking and they wanted out before any other timbers would collapse.

In the open, Mica was incredulous. "Where did you get these guns? Why didn't you use them?"

Harrison grimaced, "We couldn't get to them during the aftershocks, and the looters attacked us while we were trying to find everyone. Now, with your help, we'll be able to use them to return our people."

Having watched Theta and Slade handle the one long rifle between them, Mica was careful with these tools, these weapons. Nhe knew what they could do and was glad to have the little arsenal.

Noral and Savot were equally impressed when Harrison and Mica added their cache to the stash of weapons on the floor of the shelter. Logistically, they had two rifles plus Theta's, one hand gun, Slade's bow and arrow. Mica found a metal pry bar, Deenam had a blacksmith's sledge hammer. Landon could use the shotgun, Bauer and Stirling carried farm implements, a pitchfork and shovel. The large butcher knife belonged to Alpha.

Depending on the intelligence Theta would bring, Noral and Savot both favored a surprise element to their approach to the brigand's lair. Bauer and Stirling used sharpening stones to refine the edges of their tools. Harrison and Landon secured ammunition to match with weapons, and Deenam practiced swinging his heavy hammer at different heights and angles. It was formidable and Deenham became comfortable with it in his hand.

While they talked, Adrion's hands twisted and prepared twine.

"Adrion, I have something you can have for the next part of your journey." The station master had been watching Adrion and appreciated the youth and curiosity he saw in nem. Some of their finest young adults were killed or kidnapped. Harrison did not want a similar fate for Adrion. "Here," he said and handed the uniale a powerful but lightweight ax. The hardwood handle was smooth but contoured to the touch. The axe head was sharpened. "It's nicely balanced, with the right swing, you can fell trees."

Adrion was surprised and nhe gratefully accepted the gift without hesitation. "I... I— thank you!" Nhe couldn't take eyes off the treasure in hand. Nhe looked around and saw smiles. Nhe was given a valuable tool.

Quickly nhe moved to an open space to handle the

axe and swing it at some laying logs. The grin on nes face satisfied the station Master who shared a smile of his own.

Scouting the encampment of the slavers meant days of silence. Slade and Theta were synchronized to their purpose. The rifle was taken with them, its weight shared by passing. There were only the sounds of forest animals and a breeze in the trees. Except for their task, it could have been a pleasurable walk in the woods.

The two moved quickly in the supposed direction the looters took weeks before. The brigands had no worries about being followed and dragged their captives towards their cabin. Even now the carelessness of their trail was evidenced to Slade's eyes. In places, the brigands used deer trails, in others they bashed through undergrowth. Seeing the direction towards the hills, Slade stopped. Nhe would go around the hill to survey the camp from a different angle. With hand signals, nhe and Theta parted, each taking a serpentine route, each quietly deliberate.

At night, Slade and Theta stayed awake watching the encampment from the cover of the forest. They marked the number of the enemy, the location of the captives, and the laxity of the night watch. With disdain for the Station people, the looters never considered a rescue attempt after this much time.

With a few hours of sleep, Slade and Theta again spent the day evaluating the cabin area. There was one huge man who always yelled loudly. Two men were evidently his back -ups and the rest, fourteen of them, just followed directions. There was no indications of hunters or scouts being away from the compound, always a possibility. There was no safety perimeter. This second night offered a few changes. Two of the brigands went to the captives' cave to bring a uniale and a woman back to the cabin. Slade could hardly restrain Theta from charging into the cabin alone. The muffled cries and laughter died down with the loud man's yell.

Pulling Theta away, Slade started back to the Station. Slade took an alternative route as nhe carefully marked the trail on trees in places no one but nhe would see. This would be the approach for the rescue. The physical activity helped assuage the tension of watching and listening to the looters.

Far from the camp by nightfall, Theta and Slade relaxed just a little. They could speak in quiet whispers and briefly forget the events seen. As they lay together, the crystal sparkle of stars above the forest darkness reminded them both of the beauty of their surroundings and they could comfort each other with loving touches. Danger and affection became shared emotions.

At dusk, on the fourth day, Slade and Theta returned to the station as quietly as they had left. They had scouted the lair over two nights to find weaknesses and strength. Different individuals were identified, habits recognized. A staging area near the camp was determined. The safety of the captives was paramount.

Into the night, a strategy developed. The surveillance information assured the planners the mission could succeed. Sleep was sporadic, there was too much anticipation.

26

It took most of the day to traverse the distance to the Slavers camp. Going uphill was difficult for Noral but nhe insisted on staying with the group. Nhe was frustrated with the thought of slowing everyone down. Being crippled did not bode well. From the earthquake killing friends, to being broken in a flash flood, being held prisoner and drugged, and now struggling to travel, Noral was compromised and nhe hated it. Anger fueled determination, and this would be nes fight as well as theirs.

The group were stealthy moving through the forest. The serpentine route disguised the band and they arrived at a sheltered area near a stream whose gurgling waters drowned out small sounds. Their plan of surprise would fail if the animal life sounded an alarm they were coming. Slade's route took them around the sight line of their enemies' stronghold. It was not a fortress but located next to a rockface protecting the back of the roughhewn cabin. The cave where the captives were kept was next to the cabin with an iron gate holding them prisoner.

There would be no campfire, but the spring night was mild. An overcast sky forecast possible rain in the morning. Noral drew their plan on the ground in the fading light and one by on the people whispered their part in the coming day. Night watch was set and through the darkness, Theta and Slade set their traps along possible exit trail from the brigands' compound. When Noral gave everyone direction to get some sleep, the fatigue of the day promised a fragile slumber.

At dawn, a large uniale came out of the cabin door, stretching nes arms and scratching nes body. Rubbing a bald head, nhe yawned and lumbered over to a worn path leading to their waste creek. Nhe was still sleepily holding nemself, urinating into the water, when a hammer knocked the bald head from behind and the body slumped. Without a sound, Deenam grabbed the uni under the arms and dragged the still figure into the bushes, covering the body with more forest litter.

Another man emerged and crouched at the smoldering fire in front of the cabin. He rubbed his flannelled arms to create some warmth, but his attention was drawn to movement in the berry bushes toward their creek. *Probably a racoon trying to steal tidbits from the fire pit*, he thought to himself. He paused, then rose very slowly. The racoon didn't show itself. He moved slowly towards the bushes, then halted. Racoon meat wasn't very tasty, so he decided not to pursue it and turned his back. Stirling's arm surrounded the man's throat like pulling down a frisky foal. With a snap, the neck was broken, and Stirling quietly pulled the man into a nearby shed.

The people in the cabin were still waking up. As complacent as the slavers were, the lone night watch was asleep under a lean-to and no alarm was given. He changed his position a bit, snorted, and started snoring as Bauer approached the shed. The snoring stopped abruptly with the dull thwang of metal as Bauer's shovel smashed into the sleeping face.

When the first uniale did not return, a uniale came out of the cabin door. Making his way through the forest to the waste creek, nhe pulled down grimy pants and seated nemself on a log over the creek. Nes buttocks extended over the water, and the log was perfectly located. Nhe was uncomfortable and began to strain. Nhe looked down at clenched fists and was so occupied when the blacksmith's hammer hit nem on the side of the head and the force carried nem over the log into the creek below. Nhe floated briefly, then snagged on some branches, and lay there not moving.

There was a pause. None of Noral's band could see the others, they weren't sure how many of the renegades remained. The morning silence became unbearable as tension rose. The cabin in front of a sheer rock face and cave were an excellent defensive position. Before the cabin, a fire pit was dug near a workspace with the shed where Stirling had dragged the man. Opposite the fire area was a well. Theta perched in a tree overlooking the open space, with Slade concealed in nearby brush. Deenam and Bauer waited between the cabin and the waste creek. Savot and Alpha hid near the captive's cave. Harrison lay poised next to Alpha with his rifle. Landon was there, anxious to free the captives. Noral stood in tall sword ferns just to the side of a cleared walkway toward the cabin door. Adrion stood nervously next to nes parent with Mica beside them.

A woman's scream shattered the silence. Then another. "Delyth!" Landon said through clenched teeth. He started to run to the sound but Harrison caught him.

"Hold to the plan, just a few minutes more," Harrison whispered tightly.

"Hello, inside! Come out!" It was Noral now standing with nes crutch in the clearing leading to the cabin. Nhe reminded nemself, "The leader, finish the leader."

"Who are you?" a rough voice yelled from inside. "What the gowno are you doing telling me what to do!"

Noral stood nes ground but nodded imperceptibly towards the back of the cabin where two figures were creeping around it. The movement was identified by Slade standing in the brush near the perimeter. Nes two arrows in quick succession stopped all movement there but voices in pain remained.

"All right, you slimy crippled uniale, I'll come out." The door swung open and a huge man wearing a bear skin and fur hat filled the doorway. "What do you want?"

"We want our people, the ones you took from the Station House. We want them now!" Noral's voice was clear and demanding.

"You and who else?" the bear laughed. "You don't look much like someone who could take what you want." He quickly surveyed the open area to see the placement of this stranger and location of his own men. Leaving the doorway, he moved forward so others could exit around him.

There were four mixed ruffians beside the biggest and movement at a window alerted Theta. Slade slipped nes bow to nes back and picked up the gun from Harrison's cache. Nhe also aimed it toward the cabin where morning light showed a gun barrel searching a target.

Holding the crutch, Noral started to walk towards the cabin, towards the man. "I want them now!" A gunshot from the cabin narrowly missed Noral who kept walking and said again, "I want our people!"

Theta returned the gunfire immediately and there was no longer a threat from the cabin window. She sent no hail of bullets, ammunition was too dear. The gunshots made the standing outlaws dive for cover and two brought out hand guns to fire back. Slade and Theta reduced the men in the clearing by those two.

Again, Noral repeated the demand and this challenge from a uniale triggered rage in the man who screamed and ran towards Noral with a raised hunting knife. For size and weight, his charge was surprising! Noral stood on both legs, raised the crutch and swung the wooden rod with such force that the knife was deflected before nhe was even reached. The huge man was startled but spun around and lunged again. His scream of anger sprayed spittle as Noral prepared with another swing of the staff. There was a loud crack as Noral's blow shattered the knife wielding arm. Noral shoved the opponent off balance with the end of the crutch and the flailing man fell.

Noral had never felt such anger before. All reason and uniale discipline disappeared with the adrenalin flush of defending nes own life. Feeling no pain, Noral stood over the lumbering giant and used the crutch in hand to beat the man again and again, until the wood splintered. The protection of the bear skin let the screaming man take his knife in the other hand as he struggled to rise when Noral jumped on his chest and drove the splintered wood into his throat.

The man looked startled, then coughed, and finally whispered, "Oh, gowno!" as blood spurted from his throat and mouth.

Brigands swarmed out of the cabin. They spotted the source of gun fire and arrows and moved towards the trees. From a lean-to at the back of the cabin three of the gang ran to the open space with their knives. Deenam rushed to the ferns, grabbed Adrion, and pulled nem next to him so their backs were at a large tree. They defended themselves with the blacksmith hammer and axe when a slaver with a hatchet charged them and sliced at Adrion.

Noral was off balance and struggling to get off the bear of a man when Theta clambered down the tree to stand next to nem with her rifle. Slavers began to circle them and when one rushed forward, she pulled the trigger. She didn't pause with the knowledge she had just killed a man. She re-cocked the lever action rifle and aimed again. The slavers stopped immediately. They spun and ran for cover.

Mica ran towards the cave where nhe could hear cries for help. One brigand tried to stop nem and was downed by the swing of the crowbar in Mica's hand. Immediately, Mica aimed the bar at the iron gate keeping the prisoners in the cave. As Mica worked to release them, one of the captives screamed pointing behind Mica. Before nhe could react, a knife slashed Mica's shoulder. Nhe twirled and swung out with the bar then heard a blast of a shotgun as Landon finished the slasher. Landon took the crow bar and finished opening the gate calling "Delyth! Has anyone seen Delyth?"

There was more gunfire and then silence but for

moans and curses. The few remaining slavers ran into the forest. Cries of pain were heard when a runner stepped into a trap. Many of them would not recover. They would not terrorize people again.

The band looked about, they were all still there! Mica was bleeding from the knife slash. Stirling and Bauer had defensive wounds on their arms. In the excitement, Adrion didn't notice the gash on nes leg. The wound would have crippled nem but Deenam had deflected the aim of the hatchet strike.

As the captives came out of the cave, Landon repeatedly asked for his daughter. One uniale nodded toward the cabin and Landon went into the dank and smelly hovel. "Delyth?" Landon called. He heard a whimper from a corner but there was little light to see the figure crouched into a tiny human. "Delyth, it's me," Landon said, gently holding out his hand. "It's all right now." The girl didn't move, she just whimpered.

Landon sat down on the floor and reached toward the girl, mostly naked and dirty. "It's all right," Landon crooned as he wrapped his arms around the trembling girl and pulled her onto his lap. "It's all right, beautiful Delyth, your Papa is here." And he rocked her gently, as he held her tight.

In front of the cabin, people were already pulling the dead and wounded away. They were unceremoniously dumped into the now vacant cave. The captives were weakened, filthy, and very thankful for their rescue. They were also surprised to be saved by outsiders. Some wept in Harrison's arms, and Alpha held two children. They had given up hope. With Stirling and Bauer, the released people kept patting the strangers and grabbing their hands in gratitude.

Adrion sat with Savot and Alpha as they cleaned and dressed wounds of their people and the captives, including nes. Looking about, Adrion saw Noral sitting alone. Nhe was in shock and Alpha nudged Adrion, "Take one of these blankets to your una, nhe needs you."

Adrion quietly approached Noral sitting with nes back to a tree and nhe was shivering. Adrion pulled the blanket around nes parent and sat close. The rage and anger in Noral quieted and gradually the trembling stopped. Emotions were controlled. Someday, nhe and Adrion would talk about today, but not now. Nhe took Adrion's hand as they watched their people taking care of each other.

Food was a primary need, the rations given the captives were very sparse. In the cabin pantry, foodstuffs were devoured eagerly until the empty stomachs were partially content.

The evening rain held off and people were able to sleep outside with a minimum of protection. No one could tolerate the rancid, sour smell of the cabin or cave.

Adrion left nes una sleeping from exhaustion and moved to the circle near the fire. Deenam kept close watch for Noral and would rearrange the blanket if the uniale tossed or turned.

"Why would people like these slavers do this to other people?" Adrion asked Savot as they shared some jerky.

"Questions! Always with the questions!" Savot laughed lightly. "Don't you ever get tired of asking why?"

"Don't you ever get tired of answering them?" Adrion asked with a smile.

"All right. An answer. I don't know! There are stories of people enslaving others throughout human history. It seems to me that when one people gets strong enough, they enslave the less powerful people. There seems to always be a reason, a justification to control the lesser people. Whether its small bands or huge empires, the need for power seems to be constant."

"We weren't like that in Deerwhere," Adrion offered.

"Oh, no?" Savot questioned. "Think of how Deerwhere enslaved the drones to do the dirty... or *undesirable* work in the Colony. Think of how we humans were enslaved to do the work for Keeper. With Keeper, it didn't conquer humans, instead we gave total power to the Quantum Computer. Slavery is a complicated concept. It's all tied into the need for power, dominance. Maybe it's a gene we don't understand, 'The Power Gene.'"

27

The moods of the captives and rescuers were elated as they packed the few supplies they could carry home to the station. All the found tools from axes to hammers were packed onto a travois to be dragged through the forest. The rifles and hand guns were added to Harrison's cache. Except for two.

Harrison selected two finely kept rifles with ammunition and said, "I think Noral and Slade should keep these. They definitely know how to use them and will use them well." Slade accepted the gift with the same smile as Adrion accepted the axe. Noral hesitated as nhe never handled a gun before, but seeing it used for hunting and defense, nhe appreciated its value. Nhe took the gun gingerly as Harrison added, "And we know a little female hunter who will teach you how to use it!" People standing near stopped their preparations to laugh. Theta beamed and nodded. Tools and weapons were of paramount importance in this post-earthquake world.

"One more thing," Deenam added. "I haven't had time to carve another crutch for you, Noral, so you'll have to get by with this cane made from a root." He held the short rod out, never looking away.

Noral took the cane and made a playful swing with it but was glad it came from Deenam. "Thank you," nhe said, "I'll try not to be rough with it."

The dappled forest light added to the good humor of the people going home. Birds were fluffing the feathers and calling songs while squirrels chased each other to find mates. Slade and Theta checked the traps they set on the cabin trails and removed snares dangerous to wildlife. They found two traps that showed blood and human releases. The scoundrels were not there but now they were injured and not threatening. Still, Theta and Slade kept watch over the little band returning home.

Noral walked at the end of the troupe keeping pace with Landon and his daughter, Delyth. She was very frail and injured and it would take much time and attention to repair her damage. She would not be separated from her father and he held her protectively. Avinir, a uniale who was also abused, kept them company. Walking with these people assured Noral nhe was right in the fury which overcame him. The brigands destroyed young lives and fractured families. The pain they caused would not heal and nhe reconciled nemself. At first surprised by the depth of the anger, Noral now accepted responsibility for nes actions.

With the late start and injured, the day walking extended, and a night stop was chosen. Slade and Theta kept watch and Adrion joined them. They did not expect problems, but they would not relax until they returned to the station. Noral and nes small group joined the others for a restful night. Of all the hazards and disappointments of these last weeks, Noral admitted to nemself the pride felt in Adrion's maturity and Deenam's returning attention.

Step by step, each getting closer to the Station House. By midmorning, Noral, Landon and their lagging party reached a small meadow with a pond. With the clean air, nature sounds, and gentle breeze it was a reminder of the forest before it was wrenched into chaos by the earth's plates shifting. Noral stopped to take a mental picture.

"It could be a 'perfect pond' couldn't it?" said the masculine voice behind nem.

Noral smiled. "I was just thinking the same thing." Nhe turned to see Deenam.

"Well, I just happen to have a few stones here, we could try them out." Deenam handed three round stones to Noral who took them and rubbed them in nes fingers. They felt cool and smooth.

"Here goes!" Noral laid down nes pack, took a stance and threw the stone in a skipping motion. It did not skip, it just sunk at the first hit, ripples spreading on the smooth water. "Hey, I'm out of practice," nhe laughed.

"Excuses, excuses, old man!" Deenam said with a condescending tone. "A true stone skipper never loses the talent! Let me show you." Deenam took a stone from Noral's hand, poised himself and threw the stone at the pond. The stone skipped once, twice, and then, it too sunk into the water.

"Okay, true stone skipper, it was a good try, but I have my powers back. Stand aside." Noral made grand motions of pushing Deenam aside. Landon watch the two puzzled by what they were saying. "Watch this!"

Noral said as nhe let lose the last stone.

The stone skipped once, twice, three times and landed on the opposite shore. "Aha!" cried Noral.

"Aw," lamented Deenam and the two laughed, wrapping their arms about the other's shoulders.

They had done it, a perfect skip at a perfect pond. It didn't matter if it was a small pond after years passed. The uniale and man stood smiling at each other, then Deenam left to join the forward people. Noral picked up nes cane and pack and continued with nes slower companions. It was a perfect day at a perfect pond. It was all that mattered.

The excitement of the return of the captives was exhilarating. People could not talk fast enough to express their exuberance. Chores were temporarily set aside to create safe places for the returnees to lay down, rest, visit with families.

When Noral and the last of the injured stragglers walked into the Station the people became silent. Delyth and Avinir were but two of the injured and the price all the recovered paid was evident in the pain in their eyes.

Sensing the quiet, Alpha started gathering people and encouraging them and fussing to make sure each captive was re-united with someone. There were still aftershocks, but shelters were erected out in the open with slanted roofs to allow the rain to channel away. Outdoor kitchens prepared warm meals. She was everywhere directing and helping. Blankets and linens cleaned of earthquake dust were wrapped around the weary travelers. Tubs of warm water waited behind modesty curtains to bathe sore limbs and exhausted spirits. The Station people were re-establishing their claims on this particular piece of earth and now the beloved captives had returned.

Deenam came into the station area carrying packets of foodstuffs from the cabin's larder. He took it to the outdoor kitchen where wood fires were being stoked and gave the packets to the cooks. All the while, his eyes were searching for Bronwyn. In the excitement of the return, no one seemed to know where she was. He caught Alpha by the arm and asked, "Where's Bronwyn?" She smiled and pointed towards the clearing in the woods.

"Bronwyn, we're back." Deenam said tentatively, seeing her sitting on the log.

"Oh, yes! I know. I could only get a hug from mother and father before they took over telling everybody what to do. I'm not much help right now." She stood and he could see the baby was more prominent and birth was imminent. "I'm just trying to stay out of the way. Oh Deenam, your people were wonderful! You brought everybody back! You made us whole again." She wobbled to him and took his hands in hers. Strangely, she raised them to her lips and kissed them. No one had ever done that before. He did not know how to react. She looked at him with honest admiration and said, "Thank you, from the bottom of our hearts."

28

>>MOLLI Insert<< The industry around
the Station was amazing to anyone who
stopped working long enough to watch.
With the return of the captives, all
spirits were raised. There were
appropriate burials and last rites as
needed. A cemetery was marked for
special remembrance. The horses and
livestock were rounded up and corralled.
Families kept close and toiled together
as if afraid to be separated again.
Debris was sorted, repaired, recycled or
destroyed. Emphasis began on the water
supply and cheers went up when the town
well pump spurted out its first clean
water. The resources were at hand, the
people just had to work for them.

Clean wash began to appear on clothes
lines, just a few at first, but it
demonstrated a promise of more. The
children who had been secreted away were
again running and playing.

Always, there was a fire at night,

sometimes near the Station House, other times near a collapsed dwelling to get rid of the damaged materials. It was a comfort to sit with friends and family, be warm, and watch the flames dance. It was an ancient tradition now having renewed purpose. The modern world of autotrains, computers, and genetic hybrids renewed a loyalty to campfire.

Food remained a concern. It would be long before the summer berries and tilled crops could provide for the people. The forest new growth over the last centuries should support the community. The hunters went into the woods to bring back the wildlife flourishing the last centuries. The Station settlement was always a frontier way station instead of a colonial city. People who drifted away or preferred the roughness of the area settled there. They could sustain themselves, they could survive.

Upon the return, Noral and the others eased into the community life. They were rescuers and treated as such. It took some days for them to feel fully recovered from their wounds. Working with the others helped stretch injured muscles and nursing attention improved the healing of cuts. Some of the bruises turned yellow and started to fade. There would have been contentment with the days, but a nagging thought kept returning. What happened to Deerwhere? The Station House was returning to life after the earthquake and brigand attack. Was Deerwhere?

Looking at the fire, Noral surveyed nes small group.

Adrion was growing so fast, nhe matched nes una's height. Nhe had the self-confidence of a grown uniale, was no longer a "whiney" little bril. After all, Noral grinned to nemself, Adrion could wrestle a cougar with bare hands. Confidence. That was a common virtue in the people around Noral. Theta could lead or follow and showed compassion for her mates. Slade was still a bit mysterious but nes loyalty and willingness to sacrifice for the band was undeniable. Mica grew in skills at every occasion and was totally reliable. Savot? Savot was Savot was Savot. The heart and brains of the excursion. And there was Deenam, possessing all the qualities of a good man.

There was movement at Noral's shoulder and nhe turned to see Adrion holding out a stick. "What's this?" nhe questioned taking the stick in hand.

"It's your drawing stick. It's time to go home." Adrion smiled and Noral started sketching in the sand as the others joined them.

When everyone else left to sleep, Noral and Deenam sat looking at the flames. "I wonder if people stopped talking to each other when open fires were banned," Noral said thoughtfully. Without thinking, nes stick continued to draw little circles in the sand around the fire pit. "I wish you were coming home with us, Deenam."

"It was a hard decision, much harder than I thought it would be. I'll watch you all get ready, packing, repacking, sharing. I may want to go with you, but I know now that my place will be here."

"It's the baby, isn't it?"

"Only part of it. For all we've done together, this station feels more like I belong than I ever did at

Deerwhere. The men, women, and uniales have purpose. And there's the baby." A warm smile came over his face. "We just returned when I attended the birth. It was something to be there for Bronwyn. You know, you've had a baby yourself."

Nhe shook nes head.

"Whew, I knew birthing a baby was hard, I just didn't know how hard it was to *watch* someone have a baby! I held her hand as she puffed and pushed and screamed and pushed! One time Alpha yelled, 'Deenam, Breath!' I was holding my breath while she pushed and all of a sudden there was a beautiful, perfect little girl in Alpha's arms. We all laughed with joy, even Bronwyn."

Noral shook nes head in amazement. "Isn't it strange that I led a revolt so I could have a baby of my own while you are choosing to stay and raise a baby not your own. I wanted all Adrion has turned out to be—someone who looks like me, acts nes own way, and I can love. I made the choice because the desire to be an una, a parent, was so strong I couldn't deny it."

"Maybe you were directed by your biological clock, and I am listening to my heart. I have feelings for a child who can be more than I am."

"Maybe it is the matter of choice." Noral said pensively, again staring at the fire.

"It is a puzzlement." Deenam agreed. "Perhaps, I am making this choice for the same reason. It's what a man does. He chooses to take care of those who need him."

"Are you sure about this?" Theta asked, putting her hand on Deenam's arm as the travelers were leaving the station. "I know I get grouchy as times, but if I have to be

mugged in a forest, you're the one I want to be with."
She returned his smile at the memory and scuffed his full
beard. "With all that's happened, it seems a long time
ago, doesn't it?" She reached up her arms and hugged
him around the neck, then quickly looked away.

"Yes, I'm sure," Deenam said looking where Bronwyn
stood with the new baby who was praised and cuddled
and passed around the folks coming to say goodbye.

Harrison watched the packing activity and suggested,
"You could all stay. We'll make room, we want you." He
rubbed his arm awkwardly as if not knowing what else to
say.

Noral pulled on nes pack and held up the twisted
cane "I don't know when I'll need this cane again, but I'll
think of you when it's in my hand. Take care of yourself,
Deenam, I don't want to lose you again."

Seriously, Deenam answered, "You won't." The man
and uniale paused, looking directly at each other and
then Deenam laughed, "Besides, you'll know where I am.
Just follow your drawing stick and come get me!"

"Come on, come on, we've still got daylight if we get
our hugs, tie up our packs, and get going. Take care of
your new family, Deenam." Savot patted the man's
shoulder and looked to where Bronwyn was standing
with the baby. She waved and smiled at the uniale who
still wore the recording helmet.

More hugs and handshakes and new steps were
taken to return to Deerwhere. The steps seemed more
real, the direction more certain. They were going home.
Deenam was already there.

They were making good time on this hike. The successful
return of the captives and the respite found at the
Station House encouraged everyone. The lengthening

day light hours urged them to cover territory. No longer searching for tracks or traces of autotrains, the group followed the direction North. Terrain was familiar, and the forest was no longer formidable. They had good news in the possibility of computers online and there was certainty other people, good and bad, survived the earthquake. Deerwhere survival was now possible in spite of losses.

Rather than skirting the ghost city, the travelers walked into the streets. There were noises of wild life and creaking buildings. Adrion was cautious in nes approach to the main avenue but intrigued by buildings there. Everyone fanned out and examined some of the broken windows and doorways to stores filled with products or completely stripped of merchandise. Drawn to one commercial building by the display of camping merchandise in the broken windows, Adrion was disappointed when pulling apparel off a rack. Rotted clothing fell apart in hand. Nhe had been growing these weeks and needed to find something to replace worn ragged clothes. Nhe moved through the dusty aisles until hearing a movement just at the edge of vision. Turning quickly, there was a glimpse of something big and brown. Now unseen, there was a crash as if the large figure banged into some counters or furniture. Adrion froze in place. Nhe could hear heavy breathing, then realized it was nes. Never taking eyes off the shadow left by the figure, nhe started to back away. Nhe released the axe from the strapped case at nes waist and held it ready. A few more steps and nhe would be in the open. A blood curdling growl came from the dark figure standing huge and upright in the dusty light.

Adrion turned to rush for the door, when the floor

collapsed with nem falling through debris to the floor below. Boards, dirt, and rubble fell on top of nem.

Stunned, Adrion tried to locate nes limbs to see if nhe was intact. Nhe looked up to see a horrible head with a huge maw snarled again in the opening above. Teeth flashed in the dim light. It was up there, nhe was down in the hole. With courage that surprised nem, and the protection of a collapsed floor, Adrion stood to nes full height and waved arms and screamed. The growling head pulled back from the hole but Adrion kept screaming and waving the axe.

Nhe didn't stop screaming until Savot peeked over the hole. "Adrion, what is it? The floor just collapsed, are you all right?"

Seeing Savot turning so the helmet recorded the dimensions of the hole, Adrion wanted to stop screaming but couldn't! "Savot! Savot! Savot, watch out! It's there, it will kill us both!"

Savot attempted to calm the uniale, "It's gone, there's nothing here. It's all right." By then Noral and Slade were bending down looking at Adrion in the hole. Because of nes terror, they stood to do a quick sweep of the floor but found no monster. They did find some metal racks to lower to Adrion to get out of the hole.

When Adrion scrambled to the first floor, nhe looked to where the shadows disappeared. "It was there, huge and brown pelted, with enormous teeth. It roared at me!"

The three uniales looked at the younger one and attempted to hold back grins. Savot worked to get a straight face and said soberly, "You know, Adrion, there is a legend, a myth in these north woods about a huge man-like animal. It's been called Sasquatch or Bigfoot, and you may have just encountered it as well!" With that comment, no one tried to restrain the laughter! Adrion stormed out of the building with anger and embarrassment.

29

Wait! Adrion Wait!" Savot called, trying to catch up to the runaway. "It's all right! We just found you in a hole and thought it a... bit unusual. Calm down and be careful what you explore."

Adrion straightened to regain some composure, replaced the axe in its holder and allowed Savot to change the topic. "What are we exploring? We went through here before and didn't really find anything."

"We're looking for ancient electronics. We know some of them are still active and there were transmissions from Deerwhere to Bethid's compound. Remember the dish on top of Bethid's tower? It may have been connected to a geosynchronous satellite."

"Wouldn't the quake have disoriented the dish, changed its perspective?" Adrion questioned, now interested.

"That's why we need to get back to Kalen. Nhe understands all this better than I do." The next thought was interrupted by an aftershock, stronger than others.

Small tremors almost went unnoticed, but this shock lasted long seconds. The traveling party ran out to the streets but watched the buildings to see which were cracking anew. A precipice falling from a tall building was barely avoided and they scrambled to a street of rubble from structures already flattened.

Small animals escaped their hiding places and leaped about the broken edifices. Rats and squirrels ran out of old spaces and disappeared into even tinier new holes. Feral cats were not too frightened to miss the opportunity to hunt and many a rodent did not find new shelter.

"Are we okay?" Theta checked their number. "Are the shocks getting worse or are we just more vulnerable?" She kept her arms outstretched for balance as did the others. They hesitated to hold the shards around them preferring their own balance on the moving ground.

"It's this town. Buildings always collapse worse than the forest," Mica said, never taking nes eyes off the few surrounding walls. Sounds of structural collapse surrounded them and they stayed in the relatively open place. Gradually, the tremor ceased, and they gingerly climbed over the street rubble and broken glass.

Standing next to Slade, Mix began a low growl. His hackles stood up and attention pointed to the edge of one destroyed shop. At the edge of a pile of bricks, a dog appearing animal eyed the canine. It was a stand-off as Mix bristled, every muscle trembling.

"Stay, Mix. Stay," Slade commanded. At sound of a human voice, the coyote turned and ran away. Mix continued to watch, not relaxing when Slade patted his head.

Watching the coyote disappear, Slade started speaking quietly when Adrion realized nhe was being addressed. "You were lucky back there at the hole and thought fast in a terrible situation. Our laughter was heaped on you in relief. You stumbled on a bear that must have been protecting cubs this time of year. After you left, I found scat although the bear was gone. This journey has been filled with fears and one way to handle them is with humor. It's still a bit soon for you but it will come." Sincerely, Slade finished, "You remind us of our own youth, our very real fears. We all have a Big Foot in our lives. It can be an unreasonable terror or a real bear to be faced." Nhe signaled to Mix and they continued down the rubble. Adrion had never heard Slade speak so many words together at one time!

"Wait, stop!" Savot cried out. "Look over there, there's a tower." The metal frame rose above the office block and angled precariously over the avenue. Swinging from holding cables was a metal dish like the one they saw at Bethid's compound. The bend of the metal support tower brought it close enough to see its rusted mesh and cracked condition. It proved dishes were around, just doubtful in their usefulness.

"Is that what we are looking for?" Noral asked.

"Yes!" answered Savot. "That might let us contact Keeper or MOLLI or whoever the Deerwhere Quantum Computer is calling itself."

"What help is it? If the confederation has deleted us, it's all a shut down." Noral did not see the connection.

"It's all there! Since the Big Quake, all we've been doing is asking questions. Why this? Why that? How? Where? Now we know the important questions to ask and may have the system to answer them! We just need to get down into the crypt and those little crumpled dishes may be the keys." Savot enthusiastically moved the recording helmet around as nhe searched for more dishes.

"I saw one two streets over."

"There was one laying with some rubble, but it was so banged up I didn't think of Bethid's dish."

"I wonder if we could get that swinging dish down."

The whole focus now became the search for metal dishes. Paying attention to precarious walls, everyone looked up to where other dishes might be. Most of those fallen to the ground were so damaged or partially buried they weren't considered for retrieving. If a likely dish was discovered, Mica or Noral would evaluate the possibility and effort to save it. Bethid's dish was intact, not rusted, and the mesh unbroken. It had been serviced. If that was the requirement for transmission, the scraps found in the ghost town were useless. One enormous dish was discovered outside the street limits. It would take work to repair but was also too heavy and awkward for this small group to transport back to Deerwhere. Savot recorded its condition and position but did not think of taking it with them.

In between milder aftershocks, everyone carefully retraced steps. The unusual sounds of falling buildings in the distance became familiar although close noises alerted them.

Discouraged, Noral called the group together. "I'm thinking about the city between here and home. It was much bigger than this ghost town and would probably have more electronics. It was virtually left un-recycled all these decades."

"But the Big One ran right through those tall

buildings, there was a reason they called them 'skyscrapers.' It would be a lot of rubble and broken glass to search." Mica's experience with recycling alerted nem to Noral's plan.

"Maybe not," Savot said aloud. Thoughts about communications triggered nes memory. "A lot of those giants were built with earthquake codes and internal cores to protect the electronics above all. The city was a leader in previous centuries, their computer campuses designed for communications. It's one reason Deerwhere grew into a colony, its proximity to such an electronic center. We had Keeper, a quantum computer, but where do you think it was designed?"

The metropolis before them was nicknamed the Emerald City in another century. To see it now in daylight, it was no longer emerald. Pea green colors of moss and algae began at the mud stains of the lower floors of the steel skeletons and creeped up walls now vacant of window glass. Avenues of mud had partially dried into a cracked pavement while various sink holes remained like festering sores. Some of the buildings had collapsed on themselves or sunk into the liquefied soil.

"Where do we begin?" someone asked, as they approached the city from the south.

A few of the arched roadways were still intact and could be climbed over, the steel girders washed by the tide. Like giant insects, twisted metal cranes were gnarled by the landings that were once part of a world port and harbor. Flecks of orange colors bled through rust. The earthquakes and tsunami had extended the waterfront into the city leaving beaches for sea life which rapidly disappeared as the travelers approached. Seagulls flew and screeched at the walkers while sea lions lumbered away. The city, the port, the populace died years before, but the Great Earthquake actually buried it, returning parts of it to the sea.

Noral warned the others about the pitfalls and dangers of walking in city ruins. The quaking exacerbated the possibilities of accidents and trauma. They had no safety equipment, were in dangerous territory without a map, looking for electronic objects that might not exist, dependent on unstable footing, and were untrained to deal with unknown hazards.

"I don't know how we can do this." Mica voiced the thoughts in Noral's head. "One reason the city was never recycled was because of its unknown, its danger." Mica's face showed complete hopelessness. Nhe had tried nes best, always supporting group decisions but now nhe was too overwhelmed by the task to even care. Nhe sighed and sat on some crumbled stones.

Noral looked around the tired people standing near. They were exhausted and facing another obstacle to home. Home. What awaited them at home? They had traversed rough terrain, been captured and beaten, gone without food, faced wild life, lived with fear, and were pushed to limits of endurance. What awaited them at home? Nhe put a hand on Mica's shoulder and sat next to nem.

It was quiet. Quiet thoughts.

A note. A musical note was heard just touching their awareness. It extended, then changed to lesser note. A haunting melody began as one note led to another. A soothing sound, a good sound. It lingered in the mind as well as the ear.

Adrion fingered the flute and gently played the only

melody nhe knew. With dusk, the music attuned to the setting sun and for a shining few seconds, the city scape turned emerald again. Fingers lifted, touched the warm wood spaces, closed the special notes and Adrion finished.

There was no fire that night. The travelers lay close to each other's warmth and marveled at the stars over the open waters. Without trees or overcast, the luminary's overhead were breathtaking.

"What does this all mean?" Savot said finally. "Could this be the unity we seek. What it means to be part of the earth and more than just an amalgam of body and soul?"

"I haven't heard the word 'soul' for a long time," Noral said to nes fren.

"Let's use 'the soul' to mean that part of us not limited by genomes. This journey to find and give help has convinced me we all have a deeper existence—a soul. Over centuries, the idea was deleted by our science and politics. Now, we have experienced it. Our little group of people have lived it and are unified by it. Being a uniale means all dimensions in a unified soul." A pause, and nhe corrected nemself. "Being human, uniale, male, female means all dimensions in a unified soul."

"Yes," agreed Noral. "I like that."

"I think MOLLI will like it as well! Goodnight."

30

The trek through the moss green city became a scavenger hunt. So close to home, there was a temptation to pick up electronic pieces or tools, or artifacts. Some items were mentally catalogued for retrieval at a time when more workers could carry the loads. Primarily, they searched the edifices for satellite dishes. Any dish intact would point the calibrated direction to the geosynchronous satellite for the particular longitude. There were many parts of the dishes on the ground. Having fallen from great heights, they were totally damaged, usually rusty, and buried under other debris. One older building shed its facade of bricks to display the inside skeleton. It was older and shorter than surrounding skyscrapers with distinctive carving broken among the bricks.

"Look there!" Savot cried excitedly to the rest of nes team. Nhe pointed up to a series of dishes still attached to the upper levels of its core. "From here, those dishes look possible!"

"Then why don't you just climb up and get them?" There was a hint of sarcasm in Noral's voice. As a Recycling Engineer, nhe could analyze all the dangers between their place next to the building and the dishes high up on a lattice of rusted cables.

Sheepishly, Savot asked, "Difficult?"

Mica answered, "Without the right harnesses, and viable cable, a re-cyc would release the dishes to crash onto the street below and the technician would fall all those stories on top of them. Yes, I would say it would be difficult." Mica grinned.

"We'd lose the re-cyc person and the dishes for an idea that probably won't work anyway," Noral concluded. The look of disappointment on Savot's face coaxed Noral to soften. "All right. All right. Mark the place, get the dimensions and if we don't find anything better, we can return here with a re-cyc team and get your precious dishes. We aren't very far from Deerwhere."

The reminder of Deerwhere's proximity prompted faster steps. Tools and artifacts were cached, meals were snacked. Each person encouraged the others to hurry. Leaving the city, Noral turned on a hill and saw the cone shaped mountain that had beckoned so long ago. Still covered in snow, it could hide in the overcast, grow foggy, disappear in the mist. In today's crystal air, it seemed to swell and be even closer than a map would show. Noral turned away and limped north towards the higher land where the farms should be, and the people.

Casually walking onto the furrowed land, a person would notice laborers in the field straightening rows and digging holes. Seedlings of a mystery crop were beginning to show themselves and would later billow into full food crops. The scene was not unlike what was left at the Station House. An agrarian society in spring planting.

One uniale stood up taller and pulled a hat off to wipe sweat from nes brow. Nhe looked at the ragged strangers at the edge of the tilled soil and in a moment burst into calls of welcome! Nhe ran to the travelers waving the hat and yelling, "You're here! You're here! Everybody, it's Noral and Savot, they're here!"

Large, strong arms enveloped the travelers as Knight exclaimed and yelled for the others. A mass of people, back patting, hugs and exclamations swirled around the returnees. They were almost knocked down by the surge of people wanting to greet them.

"Get back, now get back," Knight said finally. "They didn't come home to be smothered."

Rook, the master farmer, joined the greeting and pushed nes way to take Savot's hand. "It's been too long, so good to have you back! Come to the house, get something to eat, we've got a lot to talk about." Rook quickly noticed Deenam was absent, Noral was limping, and there was a strange uniale with hair standing with a rifle and a scroungy dog by nes side. Nhe could hardly recognize Adrion except for the resemblance to Noral. Even Theta looked hardier as did Mica. These past months were etched into the travelers' eyes. Only now were their expressions jubilant.

Being led to the farmhouse, there was evidence of the same industry seen at the Station House. Refugees from Deerwhere proper were building shelters and a large table sat outside under a shade tree. Men, women, and uniales brought what they could for hospitality to the travelers. It was sparse but accepted for its kindness. Noral suspected the travelers' diet was better than some of the Deerwhere folk.

Kalen had been contacted and came rushing to the table. "What did you bring us? What did you find out there? Are you all right?"

Remaining at Deerwhere, Kalen had aged these past months. Noral suspected that however difficult the time had been for the team, it was harder on those who stayed.

Seeing Noral's expression, Kalen suggested, "We'll talk later. We both have catching up to do. Eat! Eat!" Kalen gestured to the meager meal and nes concern was obvious to the old fren.

After the boisterous welcome, Rook started to scatter people back to their work. They would meet after evening meal and could share the trip. Before that, Kalen, Rook, and Knight wanted to know exactly what their people would be told.

Savot began the story with the crossing of the river, and village of the sea fishing people. It was a place to introduce Slade and all the assistance nhe provided them.

Nhe brushed over the events at Bethid's compound except to introduce MOLLI's possibilities and reuniting with Noral. The Station House was the final conclusive evidence that no assistance would be coming from the Confederation. Other than a warning about renegade groups, Savot skipped details about the rescue. That could be told another time.

The concern on the Deerwhere frens' faces was a worry. Kalen tried to explain the hardships Deerwhere had endured but they always came back to the hope of assistance from the Confederation. A hope now demolished.

Noral knew this attitude would be destructive and said brightly to Savot, "Tell them about Keeper. Or MOLLI, your friend."

"Keeper is dead," Kalen said solemnly. "We've lost everything."

"Keeper is alive and well and ready to help! We can't be lost when we have the greatest library in the world just waiting for us to search its files!" Savot's enthusiasm was evident.

"Keeper's interface computers are swimming in mud," Kalen said resolutely. "We couldn't take time to recover them or their electronics or the power needed to run them. The 'grid' just doesn't exist. Keeper is sunk in a crypt."

Savot clicked on the recorder helmet. In the bright sunshine, it was re-charging. "Kalen, we discovered Keeper transmitting to a sub-station near the south end of the waters. It was a back door in the fiber optic network and with access to a satellite dish. It was still operable!"

"Impossible!" Kalen's experience wouldn't accept such an idea.

"Don't tell MOLLI it's impossible, that IT is very definite about its abilities!"

"MOLLI?"

"The Multitronic Omniscient Literary License Intelligence. It is 'Intelligent Technology,' a dimensional facet of the Quantum matrix. I've been recording our whole journey and will upload to MOLLI when we re-connect to Keeper. You'll be able to explore all the details then." Savot finished with such conviction it brought a smile to Kalen's face.

"It looks like I'll be going back to computer training," Kalen said hopefully.

"What of the other search parties?' Theta asked Rook.

"The north party with Azel found some deserted relay stations, no sign of habitation. They mapped their route, but the forest up there is pretty dense. It has become old growth for centuries. Their food ran out and they returned home. We've been stretching rations pretty thin until the summer crops come in. Fortunately, the rivers are starting to clean themselves and we're looking for ways to fish."

"We can help you there," Theta assured nem and she looked to Slade with a smile. "And what about the eastern search party?"

Rook became very somber. "We don't know. They left the day after your group did and we never heard from them again. The mountain forests just swallowed them. How did your search party survive?"

"Failure wasn't an option," Theta said quietly. It was an old saying and now, she knew it was true.

31

Once Kalen knew of the possible contact with the Quantum center, nhe was eager to begin the computer reboot. Kalen conferred with the new team of Savot, and the leader of the search party to the north, Azel. Mica would be the re-cyc specialist to salvage the dish while Nard established communications with any viable interface.

Azel wasn't sure how he became a search leader. He had been a bureaucrat the years before the earthquake covered his office with ceiling debris. Remembering a training manual, he had ordered the other office workers to get to the stairs. The frightened staff had no knowledge of the stair location but followed him, the round little man who knew where he was going. By the end of escape route, Azel was a leader. When groups coalesced to search for help, people gravitated to him. On the trip north, he was used to keeping records and memorized the paths taken. He took sightings of the sun on a hand cut appliance, not realizing it was a descendent of seafaring implements. Returning to Deerwhere, Azel brought his searchers home by the route in his mind.

Nard, the technician who aided in the Keeper Shut Down, asked to be part of this new effort. The possibility of Keeper, a functioning quantum computer, was stimulating in the quake aftermath. Keeper could not provide food, but the data needed to produce it. Keeper could not provide power, but instructions of re-establishing the power lost. Keeper could not build homes, but contained the research needed to bring shelter protection back to the colonists. Not that the people of Deerwhere were "colonists" anymore. Keeper archived the data to re-establish their society.

As the team conferred, Azel fingered a weathered acetate in hand. It was marked with the search route the north group took weeks before. Azel's team had followed the edge of the Lake that swamped Deerwhere and then proceeded to the beaches of the inland sea. Reaching the salt water Sound, they turned north again until they found a large port. There were bays for nonexistent vessels and large avenues of concrete. Abandoned so long, without habitation, there wasn't much for the group to recover from the bleak buildings. Quake damage was minimal, just desertion and dried mud. A broken sign read "EVER" and the rest was unfinished. With the food running out, the searchers turned home and, using the sun's direction, took the shortest route. They pushed themselves over the terrain and were exhausted when they returned. The teams to the East and South were not there.

"Did you see any electronics when you got to Ever?" Kalen asked Azel. "It would have been a relay tower with big round dishes on it."

"There was a grid tower, but it was bent funny. Interesting, it wasn't rusted like most of the other metal we found. By then, we just wanted to get home and we didn't try to take much from the whole place," Azel explained.

Kalen looked at Nard and Savot. "We've got to go back there. It was far enough away from the quake to escape major damage. It's a relay tower that we can activate."

"I don't understand," Savot confessed.

Nard took up the narrative. "Your southern search discovered an extension of Keeper's grid pattern at the compound. Keeper was actively communicating with it through a system of fiber optics. The optical grid was able to maintain itself, underground, through the earth quake."

"How was it possible?"

"Fiber optics were designed so that the silica glass cores would prevent attenuation, or degradation of signal. This strengthening also demanded robust composition materials in the links and connectors. 'Robust' means just that, very strong as well as resilient. Computers in the trembler zone sent/received data via fiber optics. It was an underground, flexible, very strong web. Engineers put relay stations in less risky areas like the south and north of the major earthquake zone in the emerald city. The relay stations then received the data and transmitted to the rest of the digital grid. They were access points to the digital net."

"Wouldn't it be easier to just dig through the mud to get to keeper?" Savot asked.

Kalen answered, "You've not seen this mud! And we

don't want to damage the protective Quantum crypt."

"If we can reconnect with Keeper through the Ever relay tower, we can also contact the rest of the digital grid. The relay can talk to Keeper and transmit to the satellites!" Nard said.

"But what about power?" Azel asked. "I don't understand all the digital talk but I know everything electronic needs power to operate."

Savot jumped up and twirled around, tapping nes helmet as nhe laughed. "There are solar panel shards all over the place! We'll use them!"

Adrion was confused on the next move. He wanted to go with Mica and the others to a new territory but thought Noral might need nem. Nhe found nes una talking with Rook, but hesitated to broach the subject of another journey. "Una, I was talking with Savot and Mica and... well... about their journey north... and..."

Finally, Noral laughed and waved Adrion away, "Go on! Go with the others, just be careful and watch out for Big Foot!"

In spite of the similarity of trees and chopped landscape, Azel was able to direct the hike back to Ever. Adrion and Mica were well conditioned and were pushing the pace, but Azel, Savot and Nard preferred accuracy. The longer daylight hours allowed them to get close to their destination. At nightfall, Adrion and Mica began the routines that served them so well—A light shelter in case the mild evening turned to drizzle, dry wood for a fire, boughs for a pallet, and reconnaissance of the area to make sure there were no bear trails.

"Why the fire?" Azel asked. "We've only got dried food to eat, there won't be any cooking."

Mica and Adrion smiled at each other. Adrion said "You'll see."

And Savot added, "It is just our way"

Into the darkness, the firelight proved again to bring stories. The searches both north and south brought similarities and stark difference. It was still too soon to recount some of the horrors, but the frens could elaborate on fighting cougars and sighting Big Foot. Those terrors included a humorous side. Azel was shocked that Adrion had been so close to Sasquatch. Personally, he had only glimpsed the forest legend from afar and wasn't sure of his own sighting. The large, dark, man like figure walking swiftly. Azel didn't tell the others at the time, but was now relieved to share the tale. Adrion and Azel both spotted Bigfoot and lived to tell about it. And laugh about it as well!

By habit, Mica and Adrion took a night watch. They conveniently let Savot sleep through his turn. Nhe was considered an "elder" in the troupe, and they let nem rest.

Traversing the broad avenues of concrete into Ever made Adrion uneasy. It was too much like the Gathering compound. Sensing the unease, Savot said, "These abandoned military or industrial complexes are very much the same. Lucky for us."

"Lucky?"

"They were built to survive weather, war, nuclear blasts, and even neglect. In preparing for every calamity or strategic necessity, they built to last. And we've been mining them to help us last."

"Over there!" Azel called. He was pointing to a complex with a large bent tower. Hitching up the straps and equipment carried from the re-cycling tool shed,

Mica hurried to appraise the situation. Nhe stood analyzing the climb, the obstacles, and the best method of recovery. Seeing the actual tower nhe was glad Adrion was there to be spotter. The "bent tower" was more complicated than first described.

Catching up, Savot and Nard bent backwards to see the bend with the dish. "Aaahhh," Savot stumbled with words. "Maybe we should find a terminal before trying the dish."

"Good idea!" Azel agreed. He didn't remember the girders looking so precarious. "Let's check out these buildings." He, Nard, and Savot each took a likely edifice to explore, leaving Mica to contemplate.

Mica sat down on a bench of broken concrete and scanned the tower. Nhe had never climbed anything so high or old. Nhe fingered the equipment and thought of tools left behind.

"What do you think?" Adrion asked with hesitation. The adventure of this trip was becoming serious.

"I'm still thinking."

"It sure looks high. A lot higher than those metal bridges we crossed."

"Yeah, it does that."

"So, what do you think?" Adrion asked again.

Without looking at nes young fren, Mica said, "I'm still thinking."

"Everyone, I found something! Come here!" Azel was calling from an entrance to a building near the tower. He led them through a trough-like hallway. There wasn't much broken glass, but the marble walls appeared cracked, At the end of the hallway, there was a metal doorway opening to a stair landing. "Just like home!" Azel grinned and the others followed. The stairwell continued with metal door breaks until the group was far below ground level. Filtered light from solar tubes dimly marked the way. More doorways, and there was a slight buzz in the air. A massive door was sprung on its hinges and Azel stepped over the threshold into a room surprisingly well lit.

Nard gasped. Nhe recognized some of the consoles. They were the same as the quantum computers used to interface with humans in Deerwhere. "Why are these working?" Nhe questioned aloud.

"Someone forgot to turn the lights off?" Azel appreciated the chance to joke. The tower and now the computers! He was proud of himself and a broad smile showed it.

Nard approached the consoles carefully. Sometimes such cabinets included protective shields. These seemed all right and did not react to touch. No blue defense screens appeared. The buzz from the corner was the power supply, a generator designed, manufactured, and programed to last hundreds of years. Industrial batteries were a 22nd Century marvel!

32

The quake, the trials of living the last months, this last hike through the forest, was all forgotten as Nard saw the console blinking at nem. This was where nhe belonged. Surveying the equipment, the particular cabinet displayed a special seal of such material that it had resisted vibrations and moisture. It was another wonder of the previous centuries. Perhaps this was the reason they could hope to reboot Keeper.

Nard waved hands in digital gestures to access the console and looked for a keyboard interface. The gestures received no response and keyboards or touch/drawing pads were no where in this digital sanctuary.

"How will you interface with the computer?" Savot asked, walking into the room to stand next to Nard by the console.

"Savot, is that you? I thought I recognized your voice!"

"What? What was that?" Nard exclaimed. Nhe looked around the room desperately trying to find a source.

"Yes, it's me. Savot."

Nhe said, hesitating, "Who is this?" Nhe looked about, trying to determine who was speaking.

"It's me! MOLLI! You ran away the last time we talked so I've been waiting for you."

Savot's eyes recognized a small speaker/receiver embedded in the console cabinet. MOLLI had waited for voice recognition before committing to another group of humans.

"MOLLI, what are you doing here? I left you miles away at another console!"

"I'm never miles away when I communicate through the digital web. With humans, that is. Keeper and I have such a relationship, you know. When we meditate on the quantum plane, all this hardware and software is not necessary."

"No! I don't know. That's why I'm asking. Can you hear me all right?"

"Yes, Savot. That teeny weeny microphone does us both well."

"Teeny weeny?" Nard interrupted. This was not any digital dialogue familiar to nem. "Savot, who is this MOLLI? And why is it talking to you?"

"MOLLI is Multitronic Omniscient Literary License Intelligence, MOLLI for short. It is a sentient extension of the Deerwhere Quantum Computer. As I understand it, MOLLI developed in Keeper's self-conscious and considers itself to be an 'Interdimensional Digital Entity.' I don't comprehend the quantum ramifications, I just know MOLLI can connect us to Keeper." Savot finished this introduction of the IDE to the surprised Nard.

"Can I talk to MOLLI?" Nard asked.

Savot shrugged. "MOLLI, can others communicate

with you?"

"Yes, Savot. If you give a personal statement of sharing, and your Password and Axillary Security Code, you can share."

Savot immediately repeated nes password and shared with Nard's password and code.

"Savot, do you want a personal privacy statement with this?" MOLLI asked.

Savot grinned. "No, MOLLI, that is unnecessary at this point. I trust you."

Interfacing verbally with MOLLI, Nard was able to evaluate the real time status of the digital web. Interrogation was hastened by MOLLI's quantum speeds. With Savot's urging, Nard blocked the Keeper Link to the Gathering. They did not want to advertise Deerwhere reconnection to the network. Let Bethid wonder why their connection was lost. Digital diplomats could scrutinize connections later. Nard's goal was access to the archives.

While Nard worked with the console, the others explored more of the compound. It was farther from the quake epicenter and even the tsunami effect was not as dire as Deerwhere in the washbowl. More of the buildings were habitable than Deerwhere's. There was access to the sea as well as northern forests.

Azel looked at the buildings and landscape with a logistician's eyes. There were islands shielding the seaward side. Winter was coming and the population of Deerwhere needed protection. From the stories of the southern search party, there were communities that could be linked by the Northwest Sound. Without the quarantines, sea travel might be a possibility and certainly trading among villages along the water's edge was plausible. "Ever" was only thirty-four kilometers from Deerwhere. Nhe thought back over the trail they had just taken and wondered about a new possibility. Nhe could imagine the people moving here from Deerwhere's devastation.

Each day, while Nard worked diligently with the console, Adrion explored and brought possible equipment back. Nhe set traps and there were always small animals roasting over the campfires.

Azel made a detailed survey of resources and continued his thoughts of re-location. Azel and Nard both came to appreciate the respite the campfires allowed them. Nard would say goodnight to MOLLI and join the others. Savot was saving the travel log download from the recording helmet for a less busy computer time. First the contact with Keeper must be established, then the journey log could be saved to MOLLI and the archives.

Nard explained the plan nhe and the IDE designed. MOLLI was fully functional in voice interface with Nard and Savot, but only at the Ever sanctuary. From there, IDE was synchronized with Keeper through the underground net. Because the DQC complex was compromised by the flood and mud, there was no direct connection for Deerwhere to access Keeper's interface consoles. To accommodate Deerwhere communication, there would need to be an undamaged transmission dish installed at Deerwhere to link with the transmissions from Ever. It would be temporary until Kalen and the IT's cleaned up the consoles to contact Keeper directly.

"How would we transmit even if we did have operable dishes?" Savot questioned. "Kalen seemed to think all Deerwhere servers were damaged. And how many ways can signals be sent?"

"Communication signals have always been bounced around finding open bandwidth, nearby transmission towers, hard wiring, or satellite availability," Nard explained. "All we are doing here is using a link from Keeper in Deerwhere crypt through underground cable to MOLLI in Ever. There, the transmission converts to microwave to a Deerwhere dish we can install with Kalen. MOLLI found a working console in the upper stories of the DQC. Keeper, via MOLLI will help direct the process of locating the viable console. Once Kalen cleans out the debris and gets it functioning, it can be a direct link to Keeper's archives. So, we are going to use the cable net to get Keeper to tell us how to re-install its interface consoles."

"What about Keeper? It's been pretty isolated these past months. Isolated enough to extend its dimensions to include MOLLI. We can't be sure what the Gathering transmitted to it. A useful servant before the Earthquake, are we still confident of its programming after the shaking it received? There may be other dimensions besides the affable MOLLI." Savot was giving serious consideration to the project while Nard worked with MOLLI.

"It's a matter of trust, isn't it?" Nard pulled at an ear and grinned lightly.

"I guess it is," Savot agreed.

"Uh, excuse me, does this mean I still need to climb up that bent tower?" Mica asked a bit nervously.

"Sorry, Mica," Savot said sympathetically. "We haven't found any alternatives. You'll have to adjust one transmitter dish to the direction of Deerwhere and retrieve one to take back. MOLLI says all the dishes on the tower are viable so you don't have to climb the whole way."

"Then let MOLLI climb the tower," Mica said ruefully, and nhe smiled and nodded. "Good night all. We'll have a lovely climb tomorrow."

Mica had brought gear from the Deerwhere Re-cycling storage. Nhe laid it out carefully and then attached a leather harness over hips and shoulders. The belt anchored rings to secure climbing hooks. The gloves were worn but fit snugly and the fingertips were exposed for tactile sensitive fingering. Nhe even had a safety helmet though nhe never understood how it would help in a fatal fall. There was a positioning strap and carbineers. What worried nem the most were shoes. With the travels and rough forest, Mica's boots were ragged. They were all that nhe had. Nhe took some silver tape found in one of Ever's tool caches. It was still sticky in places and nhe cut it to reinforce the worst weak spots. It would have to do.

Adrion watched Mica's care and tested the strength of the straps and carbineers. They collected a bucket of tools and Adrion would follow Mica to control it from swinging on its lifting cable. There was one master harness protecting Mica around hips and legs and shoulders. Adrion cinched a lesser belt harness around hips and legs. Nhe too wore a hard hat which would protect nem from the tool bucket being raised to Mica.

"Let's go!" Mica said after a deep breath. Nhe reached, pulled nemself up by the handhold and didn't look down. Hand over hand, nhe began connecting the hooks from the belt to each change of position. One handhold, connect the hook, release the last hook and move it to the next position. When nhe was two stories above, Adrion started up behind nem. The tool bucket was on a lanyard close to Adrion and steady. Hand by hand, Mica climbed. The tape on nes boot was holding and nhe never looked down.

Reaching the first transmission dish, nhe paused. All the dishes were supposed to be viable but the bolts holding this one ripped its fastening. Removing it would have damaged it further and made it useless. Nhe made an exaggerated shake of nes head and shouted "NO!" Adrion repeated the negative to the tense spectators below.

The climb continued. Mica thought nhe was in good physical condition, but the strains of posture, heavy safety equipment, and danger were tiring. Hand over hand, connect hook, release hook, pull body into new position. The next dish was aimed toward the north and necessitated a more awkward approach. Nhe adjusted and rested briefly then tugged on the lanyard for the tool bucket. Adrion released the line so it rose into Mica's grasp. Mica used the strongest wrench to loosen the nuts carefully. Nhe looped a lanyard through the attaching plate and tied off to a girder. Then nhe released the bolts and the dish was free. Carefully lowering the dish to Adrion, Mica looked up to the next dish. Adrion continued the process of lowering the dish, then resumed his watch. Nhe followed Mica's method of locking onto the tower.

The third dish was almost aimed correctly at Deerwhere. Mica sighed and looked down to the pavement below. Nard had painted a directional arrow to show where the dish should be pointed. Pulling on the tool bucket, Mica then used the wrench to loosen the nuts. These were a bit rusted in place and Mica wished for some penetrating oil to loosen the nuts. Using the wrench handle for a lever, nhe struggled to force one stubborn nut free. It didn't move. Nhe moved again with the harness cutting into nes thigh but needed the leverage. Pressing nes hardest, the nut released, too fast. It slipped from aching fingers and fell over fifteen meters below.

Adrion was looking up and saw Mica's struggle. Nhe turned nes head just as the nut slammed into the helmet. The watchers gasped in alarm, until they saw Adrion wave to Mica and them. Mica waved briefly but went back to the other nuts and U bolts. Nhe wanted to be finished.

Bolts loosened, dish aimed, Mica tightened the holding. There was one flange nut less, but nhe tightened the rest carefully. At Mica's back, another larger relay was mounted with more double clamps. By twisting, nhe carefully retrieved a nut from it and the Deerwhere relay was secured. Next to the relay was the satellite dish which matched the second direction on the ground. Mica only tested the U-bots for security.

With a quick check over the relays, Mica paused and allowed nemself to look at the panorama from this height. The Ever concrete and buildings paled beside the waters of the inland sea, the Northwest Sound. There were forests blanketing rolling hills with spring greenery. Islands appeared in the waters in the bright sunshine of crystal air. They appeared as dark humped figures breaking the water. The range of Olympic mountains was still accented by spring snow on peaks. To the south, the volcano cone of snow shimmered. The Mountain dominated the landscape. Seeing Mica look around,

Adrion joined the special moment nhe would always remember.

Descending the tower was almost as exhausting. Mica gradually let nemself down, watching Adrion as well.

When they were both secure on the ground, Adrion removed nes helmet, waved it at everyone, and shouted, "I'm taking this home to show Nora! I was careful!" The safety helmet had a large hole and crack where the nut had bounced.

33

Traveling home always seemed easier. The goal was accomplished, and a homecoming beckoned. Azel and the others had good news as well. They brought with them a transmission dish which could easily be mounted to a tree, aimed towards Ever. Through the transmissions, Deerwhere could again be in contact with Keeper's great library of archives. With MOLLI's guidance, they could make choices. Their earth was quieting down for Deerwhere and summer was coming soon.

The lightheartedness died quickly when the north group stood atop the berm and looked down into the valley, once their home colony. In the bright sunlight, the dried mud sink hole was desolate. Cracks hinted where buildings were buried, and they could see the top of the Quantum Core building. Little had been done to clear access to the offices and computer server floors. Savot winced in pain when nhe saw where nes museum of artifacts and studies used to be. The whole complex seemed more sunken than remembered. The flooded waters were still evident in low spots and pooled even deeper close to the battered slope where they walked. Without speaking, all stopped to look at the remains of the city.

Adrion sat down on a log and thoughts competed for nes attention. Nhe spent nes whole life in the ordered society in the valley next to the berm. Nhe took for granted the three genders and the consensus attitude of the citizens. Yet now, nhe felt nhe had learned more as a human being in the last two months than nhe would have every learned in the DQC school. Nhe learned how devoted humans could be, even if for a wrong cause. Nhe saw a whole tribe surviving on the good sense they always took with them. Nhe experienced evil and its ramifications for those who would tolerate it. Nhe relished nes own maturity and acceptance into the adult world. The older ones might not agree, but Adrion appreciated the gifts the earthquake brought nem.

Azel and the others quietly walked away, not sharing their own thoughts about the city. Adrion stayed longer, then followed the rest.

They followed the berm until the path was evident to the outlaying Deerwhere farms. Adrion noticed the tracked earth only showed egress from the city. The flattened grass and moss only lay away from Deerwhere. The quiet of the former colony was as haunting as the ghost town had been.

Coming into the farmland raised spirits a little. There were people working tilling the soil with hand plows. Adrion thought of how useful a few horses would be. Others were weeding. That seemed a common occupation whether the farm was at the Station House or Deerwhere. It appeared natural now and all the platitudes about the benefits of work were proving to be true.

After greetings, the north group met at the big outside table with Kalen, Noral, Rook, and Knight.

"We brought good news," Savot said eagerly. "We found Ever in fair condition compared to... well, to some of the cities we've seen."

"And we found a working console to contact Keeper and MOLLI," Nard began. At the looks of confusion, nhe went on, "We'll tell you all about MOLLI later. The important thing is we have a console, an interface with Keeper, a working transmission in Ever and a dish we can set up for reception and transmission in Deerwhere. We even know there might be an operating console on the DQC top floor. We should be able to dig far enough into the complex to reach it and transmit through Ever to Keeper in the crypt. We might be on our own, but we have the tools to do something about it!"

Noral looked wan and rubbed nes forehead. Nhe tried to encourage the others. "Sounds like you found what we needed. I'll get some re-cyc uni's to help Kalen find the console." The attempt did not last as nhe finished, "If we have time... if Keeper's crypt holds integrity... if the crops come in... if the volcano doesn't erupt! That's a lot of 'if's.' And the really big one... if the lake stops rising."

Savot looked to nes friend and saw such weariness, nhe asked quietly, "What is it, Noral?"

"The lake. With the big quake and tsunami, the lake bed was thrust upward. That's why the Deerwhere area hasn't drained. There's no natural outlet. The waters from the hills are collecting in the new basin and Deerwhere is sinking into a lake. Eventually, it will flood totally." Noral sighed and wrung hands together.

"We've been worrying about computers and lack of quarantines, and how to meet strangers across the sound. All the while we're drowning," Azel said almost to himself.

Workers from the field and others from the farm drifted to join the group at the table. Their faces reflected the seriousness of the reality they were facing. They waited. Not sure why, they patiently waited to hear what was said.

"Gowno! What a sad lot this! An awful lot of self-pity going on here!" Adrion said as nhe could wait no longer and stood up forcefully. Nes voice spoke with such energy, nhe immediately dominated the conversation. Nhe looked around the table, making eye contact with all there and especially nes una and Savot. "If you are finished with this moaning and wailing, I want to tell you something! My name's Adrion, only born human to Noral and I can fight a bunch of cougars with my bare hands!" Nhe slammed one fist on the table while the other gripped the axe on nes belt. "I didn't just face Sasquatch, I ran it off, and why? All I could think of was returning home to you special people of Deerwhere. You are the ones who can fight off brigands, cross rushing rivers and dig through mud to bury loved ones properly. You're the people who can shimmy up thousand-meter poles to re-establish communication with the archives of a great library. You can talk silly with Quantum computers or define the reasons of life. Deerwhere people are uniales, females, and males who are loyal to their tribe, to each other, and to themselves! So, if you are so damn special, act like it!"

Surprised by the vehemence of the words, Knight

slapped Adrion soundly on the back and said, "You're right, youngster! There's been enough moping about. We can do something about everything Noral said."

"And I'm with Knight," said Rook. "For the last two months I've watched people work harder than they ever thought they could. With or without a computer, humans have resources they alone can tap."

Savot smiled broadly. "With the archives and what we've learned, Deerwhere will have the best harvest ever, come fall! We'll reclaim what we can, rebuild what we have to, and innovate what's possible!" Savot's voice was confident and hopeful.

Eyes turned to Noral. Nhe was still sitting quietly watching the faces of the Deerwhere people. Slowly, it came. Noral's frown faded. Nes face took on a new appearance. It was the biggest, most hopeful smile of all. Nhe looked at nes dear bril and was instantly thankful for all that had brought them to this point. Nhe stood, hugged Adrion and said to all, "You're right! We have a beautiful Northwest day, it's time to have a lovely... lovely work day!"

EPILOGUE

New Confederation Years 72-80

>>MOLLI INSERT<< It took me a while to write the above story of Adrion's Passage. I had to decode Savot's log and fill in some events from my own imagination. I tried, as a newbie writer, to design my story arc with the proper suspense and climaxes. If I could present you with a graphic hologram display, (in color with orchestral music) I would. However, this simple book format limits my presentation. I have to rely on printed words .

I wanted passionately to be an author and took Savot's records as a narrative for the codex you are currently reading. Dialogue was repeated as recorded in the logs or improvised from context and the personality of the speaker.

As the characters in the story became dear to me, I thought your readership might also be interested in what followed. The humans held to their goal to rebuild together.

With the Lake deepening, Azel convinced people to move towards Ever. It offered good reclamation and nearby farm land. As the Northwest Sound cleared itself of the flotsam from the earthquake and mudslides, there was great potential for traveling the Sound by boat for trade and co-operation. No longer in quarantine, the communities became interactive. It was even suggested that with some work, the area could become "Everdon", a place of tranquility and mutual respect.

Noral was more than happy to stay and work with the survivors at Rook and Knight's farm. Even the hard farm work was a relief to walking on the injured leg. Nhe has always yearned to work soil and nurture growing plants. Where nes Reclamation work was previously the means to provide resources for an ordered society, it was now a necessity for survival. People came to nem for advice and nhe felt Torad's influence. The wise, old friend was missed and Noral did nes best to continue the mentor role.

Theta and Slade began teaching the Marlowe hunters how to track animals, and care for the meat. Game was abundant from the years the Deerwhere Colony did not hunt real animals. Conservation was one of Slade's lessons to keep the wildlife preserved. They stayed the summer helping Deerwhere make the move to Ever. By the first summer's end, the word was passed to the Station House,

the Fishing village, and the Deerwhere
farmlands to attend a Marriage Potluck.
Theta and Slade would exchange vows
before their community of frens. They
would share promises beyond a
Certificate of Unification printed by a
computer. The two of them talked more
and more about returning to Slade's
village. When they did return there in
the autumn, they took three of the
puppies from Rook's collection. They
definitely resembled Mix.

Mica became a re-cyc expert in Ever,
using the skills nhe learned from Noral
and the experience of the South search
group. Nhe kept a strong friendship with
Adrion who moved easily between
Deerwhere and Ever. Their positive
attitude encouraged the community with a
motto of "Reclaim, Rebuild, or
Innovate!" They appreciated each
other's labor.

Nard established contact with MOLLI
and helped the IDE transfer archives to
Ever. Nard was delighted to finally
communicate directly with the dimensions
of a quantum computer.

Once freed of the responsibility of
archives, DQC Keeper transitioned itself
and delved into mental thoughts of other
dimensions. Quantum computers can cross
dimensions or universes without the
hindrance of time or physical
limitations. Employing nes omniboolean
talents, Keeper embarked on an eclectic
quest to achieve digital omnisciency.
Eventually, Keeper preferred the
solitude of its crypt under water. As
Molli, I slipped away from using "we" in

my relationship with the Deerwhere Quantum Computer. I did miss the companionship of Keeper as another quantum being. Occasionally, MOLLI and Keeper try to synchronize, but their interests are so varied, exchange of data is diminished. Gradually, all human interaction was left with me, MOLLI.

Savot was perhaps the most contented of all uniales. One of the Ever buildings was perfect for nem to start a museum of artifacts and objects. Nhe always felt the objects collected could trigger visual memories for nemself, and with proper training, nhe could impart those ideas to others. Especially the young.

Adrion was a bril on the day of the great Earthquake. The journey created a mature uniale with honest judgement and the vigor of youth. Nhe truly expressed nes uniale genome with instincts for enthusiasm and survival. In the communities of the Northwest Sound, nhe became a force, a human force to be admired. After all, Adrion could fight a pack of cougars with nes bare hands!

SAVOT'S COMPENDIUM

almen: humanity; humankind
auxiliary archive control: archive, old computer servers, defense com w/force field
Big Foot: legendary creature of Northwest woods
biochip: inserted at birth for ID/sometimes called Life Chip
biocuff: added at puberty for additional electronic data, removeable
body room: bathroom
bril: a child of uniale gender or undetermined
casita: small efficiency apartment
charandos: A mystery, myth or legend
CODE T: termination through bureaucratic lobotomies
compeer: uniale peer, comrade
degausser: D-Ring magnet to DE-MAGNETIZE electronics (Old system)

DQC (COMPLEX): Deerwhere Quantum Core & supplemental server Computers

Duffield's Virus: exclamation, curse words

Ever: Partial name of community north of Deerwhere

Everdon: mythical reference (Paradise, Shangri-La, Garden of Eden)

flat: larger, more commodious apartment

fren: uniale friend

gowno: exclamation, slang for excrement

Inaczej: People of village on Northwest Sound

Intermediate (Inter M): middle school. Puberty. Biocuff synched to biochip

KEEPER: PRIME Deerwhere Quantum Computer

Keeper's Stain: exclamation, curse words

Manlow's curse: exclamation, curse words

masseusiale: uniale masseur at health pool

MOLLI: Multitronic Omniscient Literary License Intelligence

nebid: uniale sexual identity, an indentation below the navel

nem: uniale object (i.e., him and her)

nes: uniale possessive (i.e., his and hers)

nhe: uniale subject (i.e., he and she)

Northwest Sound: 47.7237° N, 122.4713° W

Nursery: where infants and toddlers are raised

Omniboolean: Quantum Computer interrogation and search

Omnisciency: Quantum Computer value of all-knowing

Optical Magnet Lattice: magnetic alignment of particles to allow quantum computing

Options: three allowed for reproduction by unit uniale

OS: operating system designed by Refounders

phonometer: measures decibels of sound of fans at Games

Programmed Study Platform (PSP): study protocols after puberty designed by aptitude testing

quantums: collections of confederation computers

Sasquatch: legendary creature of Northwest woods (see "Big Foot")

self: uni inner person, special unity of self, NOT "myself" but "my self"

SL-47: beginning programming of DQC

SL-48: program reset by Kalen

syncohol: mild, synthetic alcohol

synturf: synthetic ground cover

treds: shoes

uni: abbreviation of uniale, plural = uni's

uniale: third sex , embodiment of prime male and female genomes

Uninterruptable Power Supply (UPS): back up power supply to DQC

unit dissolution: divorce

wifand: uniale in family unit

zettabyte: chip referred to quantum computers

Made in the USA
Columbia, SC
14 January 2020

86718116R00147